ABOU

MW01243023

Holly Rae Garcia writes horror, sci-fi, and thriller stories. Her short stories and poetry have been published by Trembling With Fear, Siren's Call, Bookends Review, Australian Writers' Centre, Rue Scribe, and the *Haunted* and *Isolation* anthologies. Holly lives on the Texas Coast with her family and three large dogs. When she isn't writing, Holly works full-time as a corporate photographer.

COME JOIN THE MURDER

by Holly Rae Garcia

Close To The Bone
An imprint of Gritfiction Ltd

Close To The Bone
an imprint of Gritfiction Ltd
Rugby
Warwickshire
CV21
www.close2thebone.co.uk

The characters and events in this book are fictitious. Any similarity to
real persons, living or dead, is coincidental and not intended by the
author.

Proofread by Carly Rheilan
Interior Design by Craig Douglas
Cover by Holly Rae Garcia

First Printing, 2020

Dedicated to Ryan, Kennedy and Ethan.

ACKNOWLEDGMENTS

Ryan, I couldn't have written this book without you. You push, encourage, and love me harder than anyone. Until we're seventy, anyway.

Kennedy, you never laughed at my ideas, even when some were laughable. My sweet and beautiful daughter, you are my favorite child. Don't tell your brother.

Ethan, you almost drowned in a muddy bayou when you were a toddler, giving me the idea for the most gut-wrenching loss I could think of for a mother to endure. My smart-ass and handsome son, you are my favorite child. Don't tell your sister.

Linda Mikel Hartsfield, your critiques and comments on draft four were invaluable. Thank you for instilling a love of reading, and a love of the macabre, from an early age. If anyone has issues regarding the morbidity within, see Linda.

Heather Lander, thank you for being my beta reader, accountability partner, and friend. Your critiques were spot-on and your humor helped me enjoy the process more than I would have otherwise. You are the Alpha Beta.

Haley Hwang, thank you for editing my query letter and remembering my story when talking with a publisher. A few weeks and a handful of emails later, they were reading my book. You are a rock star.

Craig Douglas and the rest of the staff at Close To The Bone, thank you for taking a chance on me, and for your patience with my seemingly unending questions. I know I can be a pain in the ass.

Members of 'Write Around the Block', writing can be a lonely venture but having you guys to bounce ideas off of, commiserate the pains, and celebrate the wins with, has made all the difference.

To all of my friends and family who understood why I didn't go do the things or see the people because I wanted to stay home and write: Thank you.

January 2020

COME JOIN
THE MURDER

1

J ames scrubbed the soggy cotton mess until his fingertips became prunes, and he wondered if the blood would ever come out. Before it was covered in someone else's blood, it had been his favorite T-shirt. He swiped it last summer from the Salvation Army down on Avenue J. The store's teenage employees were too busy jerking off to notice he was a little thicker leaving the dressing room than when he had gone into it. With the shirt hidden away beneath his hoodie, it seemed like a perfect plan until the time came to leave the air-conditioned store. Stepping out onto the sidewalk, the thick August heat had taken his breath away. Texas summers were never a picnic, but that year it was scorching, with hardly any rain. Nothing but the near one-hundred percent humidity. By the time James got to his van three blocks away, sweat had drenched his face and his chest was tight. He would have to think of a new tactic next time. A hoodie in the summer was not his brightest idea. But the shirt was a classic, a genuine Eagles Hotel California 1977 Tour T-shirt, and worth it even if he did almost have a heat stroke. It was the only thing he stole that summer that he didn't try to sell.

He yanked the shirt out of the sink and pulled the plug, allowing the pink water to circle the drain. No matter how many times he scrubbed and rinsed, there was always more blood to wash out. He couldn't believe a measly thirty-two dollars ruined his favorite T-shirt. That's all the man had on him, thirty-two dollars. James ran more hot water onto the shirt and glanced behind him. Tommy was no help, judging from the trail his feet wore on the cheap linoleum tile in their small kitchen. Shuffling back and forth in his stained tennis shoes and baggy jeans, he looked downright pathetic. A heavy sigh in James' direction punctuated every other footstep. The only thing wearing out faster than the floor was James' nerves. All Tommy had to do was watch his back, but he had screwed that up in true Tommy fashion.

James flung the ruined shirt into the trash bin and jerked a chair away from the wooden table that sat in the middle of the kitchen. He dropped into the chair and wiped his hands on his worn jeans before reaching into his shirt pocket for a smoke. When the small orange flame from the lighter licked the end of the cigarette, he noticed a maroon streak running the length of the white paper. Of *course* there was blood on the cigarette. Blood seemed to cover every fucking thing. He hadn't realized how much a man could bleed until that night. He lit the stained cigarette and snapped the lighter shut with a flick of his wrist. The metallic smell from the lighter mingled with the rusty odor of blood in the room.

"Dammit Tommy, sit down, you're giving me a headache."

Tommy stopped in his tracks. "But James, you *killed* him! You didn't say we were going to kill anyone, you just said we were gonna get some money. You didn't have to kill him. He didn't even know our real names."

"Well, we did and now it's done. Sit the hell down and shut up for a minute." He took another drag off the cigarette. "I need to think."

Tommy's arms flailed out in front of him and his voice cracked like a pre-pubescent teenager's. "What? We?? *You* were the one who killed him! I wanted to leave!"

James pulled the cigarette from his lips and watched the ashes fall into his lap as he exhaled a cloud of smoke. His mouth drew into a thin line and he pointed the cigarette at Tommy. "This shit is your fault. If you'd watched him closer, you'd of seen him trying to get away. If I'm in it, you're in it. Now sit the fuck down and shut up."

Tommy sighed as he fell into the chair furthest from James. He grabbed his inhaler from the table and sucked on it until he no longer looked like he was going to have a heart attack, then he leaned forward with his head in his hands and waited for James to tell him what they were going to do about the 'it' he had become a part of.

Thirty-two dollars wasn't enough to keep James' mama from losing her home. What a cluster fuck his month had turned out to be. How much bad luck could one guy have? Not that he cared about being fired (his boss was a prick), or about his bitch leaving (he could finally get some peace and quiet), but he couldn't even help his mama. Since his dad died, James had promised her he would take care of her, and he usually did. When he had a job, anyway. He needed money, and he needed it yesterday.

James glared at the man's wallet on the table, now empty. Tattered, brown, and curved to fit around his fat soccer dad ass, it looked like something you got on sale down at Baywood's Food Market. *Special Today! Old crusty bread, bruised apples, expired meat, and cheap imitation leather wallets.* Its contents lay scattered around the table like the useless things they were. A library card? Who went to the library anymore? Shiny, probably never used, gym membership cards. Drug store discount clubs. Family pictures mixed in with credit cards, receipts, AAA membership card, and other crap no one cared about. The credit cards tempted him, but that was the shortest route to a trip downtown. James was smarter than that. He only kept the cash. Well, the cash and the pictures he liked. Some of the photos were definitely going into his spank bank. Fat ass soccer dad had a smoking hot wife. James always did have a thing for a brunette with a pretty face, big green eyes, and a mouth that could show a guy a good time. He probably did that bitch a favor anyway, offing her old man. She was too hot for a guy like that. The kid in the picture looked exactly like the dad, couldn't deny that one. The wife could always have more kids: better-looking ones with a husband who *used* his gym membership.

He supposed it was too bad about the brat, but what was he gonna do? Bills don't pay themselves, and while his dad was a mean drunk who liked to talk with his fists, he did always say, "It's easier to take it than make it." Not that he said that anymore, but he used to.

"Well?" Tommy lifted his head from his hands and glared at James.

"God, Tommy, calm down. It's fine." James threw the photos back on the pile and crushed his cigarette out on the top one. The family picture with all three of them smiling like idiots. The soccer dad's face melted a little more with each twist of the butt and ashes fluttered down to the dry-cleaning ticket underneath.

"We handled it, didn't we?"

When he didn't hear a reply, James looked up to see Tommy frozen in place. There was white all around his little shit brown eyes as he stared at something over James' shoulder. Beads of sweat glistened off his forehead and the color drained from his already pale Irish face. James turned around to see what the hell he was staring at. The TV. The crappy little TV he found on the side of the road last week. He almost left it there, the screen was cracked all to shit, but he thought he could fix it and make a few bucks. Then that bitch took his flat screen when she moved out. He knew he should have stayed home to make sure she didn't pull any shit, but she was getting on his nerves and he had taken off. He and Tommy were in luck and shocked to find the cracked piece of shit actually worked. Sometimes it was hard to see around the deep grooves in the screen, but they could mostly tell what was going on. And at that moment, there was a lot going on.

The same little boy whose picture sat half covered in ashes on their kitchen table looked out at them from around the crack. Then another image filled the screen.

"Daaamn, it's fat ass soccer dad! Look at that, Tommy. We're famous!"

Tommy's mouth moved but only a whimper escaped. He stared at the TV like an idiot mute, scratching a mosquito bite on his arm and not stopping even when his fingertips were wet with blood. James shrugged as he reached for the remote control to turn it up.

"... and his son, Oliver Crow, were last heard from Friday afternoon when they were heading home from a day at the beach. If anyone has information on the whereabouts of the missing..."

Crow. Oliver and Jon Crow. Well, they sure as shit weren't missing. James and Tommy knew exactly where they were.

The kid was floating around the inside of his Dad's Chevy, snug at the sandy bottom of the Canal. He wasn't as sure about the dad's location. Depending on the currents, well he could be damn near anywhere.

2

Rebecca pulled the knot on her blue bathrobe tight and shuffled into the kitchen, shielding her eyes against the harsh sunlight coming through the large windows above the breakfast table.

Oliver sat cross-legged on the marble-topped island at the center of the spacious kitchen, still wearing his pajamas. He moved his sandy blond curls out of his pale blue eyes with one hand and counted eggs nestled in their cardboard beds with the other. "... nine... ten... three-teen... four-teen..." He didn't break from counting as she ruffled his hair and walked past.

Jon was at the stove, pouring pancake mix from a plastic bowl onto the hot griddle. His white T-shirt clung to his belly, accentuating the weight he had gained over the last few years. His own hair was an exact match to Oliver's, sandy blond and curly. They even shared the same cowlick at the back, exaggerated even more that morning since they hadn't taken the time to brush it before breakfast. He didn't look up as Rebecca came into the kitchen, instead focused on the batter as it hit the buttery surface and spread out into perfect circles, sizzling.

"All right, Chef Ollie, help me watch for the bubbles."

"Okay Chef dad!" Oliver scooted to the other side of the island and sat up on his knees. Very serious about his cooking, he focused on the small tan circles in the pan.

Rebecca tuned them out as she navigated around the spilled flour on the floor and towards the coffee pot that Jon hadn't bothered to start. She frowned, already knowing Jon and Oliver would leave for their beach trip without cleaning any of it up, and she would have to do it all as usual. Jon was the fun one while she was relegated to hall monitor and janitor. She grabbed the coffee from the cabinet and wondered for what seemed like the twentieth time that week, if she had two kids instead of one.

Soon the kitchen filled with the earthy aroma of fresh coffee as hot water dripped through the grounds and plinked into the pot below. Rebecca settled onto one of the bar stools, tucked a leg underneath her, and checked social media on her cell phone while Jon and Oliver buttered the pancakes before stacking them onto plates.

She glanced up from her phone and grunted, "Jon, *honey*, do we need that much butter?" She always tried to throw in a 'honey' or 'babe' when she had suggestions for him. Otherwise he accused her of being controlling or patronizing. Which she was, but it was better to at least appear to be considerate.

With his eyes still on the plates, Jon answered her. "Of course, *honey*, it tastes way better this way." He smiled at Oliver. "Right Chef Ollie?"

"Right Chef dad!" Oliver grinned as he dug another spoonful of butter from the tub.

Rebecca rolled her eyes and returned to her phone.

After eating his weight in butter-soaked pancakes and scrambled eggs, Oliver ran off to his room screaming ecstatically, "I'm gonna get my bay-bay-suit on!" His sticky hands left syrup on every door and light switch between the kitchen and his room. Rebecca grumbled as she followed behind him with a wet dishrag, wiping everything down.

It was after eleven before she could finally shoo them out of the front door. Loaded down with the typical beach accessories, they juggled cheap plastic buckets filled with Oliver-sized shovels and jars with magnifying glass lids to observe whatever was slow enough for him to catch. Tucked under Jon's arm were the last year's faded beach towels. A bag overflowed with two kinds of sunscreen, mosquito spray, glasses, hats, and extra shirts while even more toys hung from his shoulder. Rebecca helped Oliver roll a white cooler to Jon's car, letting him think he was doing most of the work. Stuffed inside the cooler were an assortment of drinks, sandwiches, and chips. Jon always made more than they needed, and of course she would be the one left to unpack it all once they returned.

If she had known it was going to be the last time she would ever see her husband and her son, she would have lingered longer and hugged them tighter. She would have jumped in the car with them. She would have stopped them from going. But she didn't know, so she only waved as they pulled out of the driveway and turned back towards the house before seeing Oliver's return wave from the backseat window.

Not that she normally would have gone with them, but her excuse that day was work. The truth was, she relished her alone time more than she cared to admit to anyone. Since Oliver was born, those moments were harder to come by and she grabbed any opportunity she could to have the house to herself. She shut the front door behind her and stood there for a moment with her eyes closed.

Silence. Blessed silence all around her.

Smiling, she was halfway down the hallway to her office when she remembered the mess in the kitchen. Of course, she could try to ignore it and make – ask – Jon to do it when he returned. But by then, the food remnants would have solidified and the whole thing would be even harder to clean up. Not to mention the fact that she wouldn't be able to concentrate on any work knowing Tropical Storms Jon and Oliver had blown through her kitchen. She turned around with a sigh. Her 'work from home' day wouldn't get to start as early as she had hoped.

Rebecca's office was small, the smallest room in the house, but it was hers. Oliver wasn't allowed to play in there, and Jon never cared about what she did. She had painted the walls a dark gray-blue color and dressed up the used desk and filing cabinet as best she could. On the walls was a collection of art ranging from Basquiat to de Blaas, all hand-picked by her and custom framed for various birthday or Christmas presents. Her favorite, de Blaas' *On the Beach* hung in a spot of honor on the wall just to the right of her monitor. In it, a young woman was pinning her hair back, standing barefoot on the beach with a basket at her feet. It wasn't a particularly striking location, or subject... but something about the solitude spoke to her.

Hours later, she was chicken-pecking the keyboard with her right hand and holding her coffee mug with her left, when Jon called to tell her they were on their way back home. She saved her progress and shuffled her papers into her monogrammed briefcase. It had been a gift from Jon's mother, Claire, when she graduated from U of H. The years had started to show on it but, thus far, Jon hadn't picked up on her hints to buy her a new one for Christmas, or Mother's Day, or her birthday. This coming August, when she turned thirty-six, she would buy the damn thing herself. She deserved it. In her short time at Waterford & Little, she had moved up faster than anyone else, and was the second youngest person ever to make manager. The first was the boss's cousin, so he didn't really count. Her chest swelled with pride, thinking back over her journey there. There were days she doubted if she and Jon would make it, there were even more days she was sure she wasn't the kind of mother Oliver needed, but there was never a day she doubted herself at work. There, she triumphed. There, she had no doubts about her performance or her future. There, she was a rock star.

She opened the pizza app on her phone and ordered their usual Friday night dinner: one large pepperoni and one large cheese, both thin-crust. She wasn't sure how hungry Jon would be, but Oliver would be famished after an entire day of running around in the sun. It never mattered how many sandwiches or chips he ate, he was always still hungry afterwards. She suspected they fed most of their food to the birds at the beach, but they always denied it.

She set the delivery time for 5:30pm, closed the app, and gave herself a pat on the back for getting a few good hours of work in and having dinner taken care of.

The phone rang again when she was settling down on the couch with a book.

"Hey babe, where did you put the spare tire? I can't seem to find it." On speaker, Jon's voice echoed through the quiet living room.

"Crap," Rebecca had never replaced the spare. Driving over construction debris (from the never-ending construction of highway 288), a nail had impaled itself in the right rear tire a few months before. Since the spare was full-sized, she never bothered with buying a new one. Of course, it didn't occur to her they would need another again so soon.

"I completely forgot to get another one. What's going on?"

"Nothing major, just a flat tire. We pulled off to the side of the bridge so don't worry, we aren't on the highway. But dammit, I thought we had the spare. Do you have the number to AAA?"

"Yeah, I'll text it to you. But I think they'll have to tow you if there isn't a spare. I'll just come get y'all."

"That works. See you in a bit then. Love you."

While there were several bridges between their home and the beach, she knew immediately which one he meant.

It was 'The' bridge, the largest one that carried you over the Intra-coastal Canal. From the top, you could see the coast stretch out for miles on either side. White-tipped frothy waves kissed the sandy beaches while darker waters waited for boaters further out. It was the best view in the county.

It took Rebecca exactly half a minute to find the AAA card in her wallet and text him the number, something he definitely could have done himself. He had a copy of that exact card in his own wallet. She rolled her eyes and put it back in her purse. Of course, it was easier for him to ask her than do three seconds of digging on his own.

In no time at all, she was heading south on Highway 332, engrossed in the latest political podcast. Podcasts were the key to her sanity during the long commutes into downtown every morning. Houston traffic gave even the most docile person homicidal thoughts. She knew she was lucky that her boss was okay with her working from home a few days a week. Rebecca (and her sanity) appreciated it. Still, she felt like she should double her output when she worked from home, so they wouldn't think she was watching TV or running errands on their time.

She was halfway to the bridge when her phone rang again.

"Hey, are you still in town? Looks like the AAA guy is here already, we'll just ride with him. You can meet us at the mechanic shop, it's closer to home, anyway."

"I'm not, but I can turn around. They got there fast."

"Yeah, I thought so too. But he's not in a tow truck. This is probably the car service so we don't have to ride with the tow guy. Either way, they really need to invest in nicer vehicles. This van looks like it's about to fall apart. I'll call you back when we're on the road again. Love you."

Later that night, she would go over this conversation a hundred times, wondering what she had missed. Wishing he had said more about the van or the person driving it. Wishing she was with them or they were safe at home with her.

Rebecca turned the car around and headed for Henry's Auto, a greasy little place right off the highway with low prices and somewhat honest technicians. It was the only shop they used, though it had been a while since either of them had needed to. They were finally making enough money to buy new cars and had done so the year before.

When she pulled into the empty parking lot, she realized they were already closed for the day. But it wasn't a wasted trip; they could always leave his car there and call in the morning to let them know what was going on. She knew the boys were still several minutes behind her, so she put her car in park and left the engine running. It was too hot outside, even in the early evening, to sit in a car without the air conditioner on. Her hand was reaching to push play again on her audio book when she thought better of it. Being the only person there after hours was spooky enough, but the high chain-link fences topped with coiled barbed wire surrounding her on three sides only added to her anxiety instead of making her feel safer. The place was a dump, but that was what one came to expect from an old auto repair shop. Vehicles surrounded her in various stages of assembly, all waiting to be made whole again. It was hard to tell if the several used tires piled by the door were waiting to go on a car or had just come off one. One benefit to using Henry's was the cheap tires. Not new of course, but would get you on the road again at any rate. A fence rattled off to her right and she heard a dog barking.

She locked the doors and rolled her windows all the way up, and muttered, "Don't worry, Cujo... I'm not coming in."

She was almost glad it had closed for the day; she

would much rather wait in her car than the waiting room there at Henry's. It was a small space, filled with two love seats that used to be shiny black pleather but had since been reduced to peeling, faded gray messes. There was always the burnt smell of reheated coffee in the air and, no matter what day you went, there would be a different version of an old man in dirty clothes trying to make conversation with you as you sat on the couch getting the back of your legs scratched by the cracked leather.

She glanced at her watch, "Shit, the pizza." No one was home to accept it. She hoped they wouldn't charge her card anyway, but they probably would. Customer service everywhere was shit lately.

The boys should have been there already. They had more than enough time to drive from the bridge to Henry's. She drummed her fingers on the steering wheel and dialed Jon's number, listening as it went straight to voicemail. She couldn't know that at that moment, less than fifteen miles away, Oliver was crying out for her. She couldn't know that in less than five minutes, he would be dead.

"Dammit Jon, pick up your phone," she grumbled.

He probably had his ringer off. That man was the absolute worst at remembering to turn it back on. She drummed her fingers on the steering wheel and listened to her stomach growling, longing for pizzas they wouldn't get to eat. An hour went by before she gave up and headed home, certain they would be there with a spare tire secured snugly to the car and already eating the leftover spaghetti from the fridge. She drove home, wondering why they paid two hundred dollars every month for phones if he wasn't going to use the damn thing.

It was a typical lazy summer evening. The sun was low in the sky, casting orange and yellow tones onto everything, whispering that it (and its interminable heat) would soon disappear. Her next-door neighbors sat on their front porch sipping margaritas while their kids ran in and out of the cool spray of a sprinkler in their front yard. Giggles and squeals floated out to the street and into her car as she rolled down the window.

"Hi Nathan. Hi Emily," she said waving to the man and woman sitting on the porch.

She was proud of herself for remembering their names, finally. It had only taken them living there for three years. She was the world's worst at remembering names. Especially those of the people she hardly ever spoke to. She was always so busy with work, raising Oliver, and the recently added marriage counseling classes Jon wanted them to attend.

Nathan and Emily held up their drinks in greeting before turning their attentions back to the kids. One of them, the youngest, had slipped on the wet grass and fallen. As she drove past, Rebecca glanced in her rear-view mirror. The kid was fine, standing up and already running back through the sprinkler. Kids were so much more resilient than you thought. They could get through pretty much anything. She remembered bringing Oliver home from the hospital and being too afraid to hold him. His little head had flopped around so much she was afraid it would flop right off. But Jon had known what to do, he had taken him from her that first night home and hadn't let go since. They were two peas in a pod. She was sometimes jealous at how parenting came so effortlessly to Jon and how much Oliver worshiped him in return. But she was mostly pleased that she didn't have to do it all herself.

The surrounding houses were all larger than her own. Their home may have been the smallest on the street, and Rebecca longed for the day when they could upgrade, but for the time being it was enough. It was a modern Victorian style, with steps leading up to a brown-bricked archway that framed their small front porch. The shutters and trim were cream, and two chimneys extended through the top of the roof. They had laughed at the idea of a fireplace in the master bedroom; during the Texas summers they practically lived on the surface of the sun. They didn't need a fireplace, much less two. But the home had everything else they wanted. A large kitchen, three bedrooms, two baths, and a decent-sized backyard for Oliver to play in. It was the perfect starter home at just under fourteen hundred square feet. A driveway ran to a recessed garage to the left of the home, and whoever owned it previously had clearly had a green thumb. Shrubberies, flowers, and trees of every color filled the small flower bed in front, and the custom beds in the back yard. Rebecca herself had never had much time or patience for gardening, so Jon was usually the one who tended to it all. The neighborhood was mostly quiet, but still contained a few children for Oliver to befriend and spend time with, when he was older and had more roaming privileges.

As she pulled into her driveway, Rebecca's brows furrowed in confusion. Jon's car wasn't there. Perhaps they stopped to pick up dinner, thinking she wouldn't have ordered pizza so late in the evening. She parked her car and stood in the driveway, eyes scanning up and down the road in front of their house. She could almost imagine Jon's car coming down the street with the windows down and Oliver's laughter spilling out.

But the street was empty.

She turned to go inside, calling him again on his cell phone.

Still no answer; straight to voicemail.

She shut the door behind her and pulled up the recent calls on her phone. There it was, the last incoming call from Jon at 5:42pm. It was almost 9:00pm. Even if he had forgotten to call her when they got on the road, they should have made it to the shop before she left. If they decided to go straight home, they should have been there waiting for her. Or, at the very least, tried to call her to say why they would be so late. Jon never thought past what he wanted to do, never thought about her plans.

"It's fine, I'm sure it's fine," she muttered to herself as she called him again.

They were probably okay.

The call went straight to voicemail again. It wasn't even ringing. His battery could be dead, or he could have dropped it in the water...

Rebecca sat at the breakfast table in the kitchen and stared at the phone in her hand. She didn't know what to do, who to call, or where the hell Jon and Oliver were. Even if his phone had died, he could have used Henry's, or the AAA driver's.

Of course.

They were with the AAA driver, she could call the dispatcher and see where they were.

She gazed at the paint peeling from the kitchen cabinets while she waited on hold for a real person to talk to.

"Yes, hello. This is Rebecca Crow. You guys picked up my husband a few hours ago and they still haven't made it home. Can you see if they went to a different shop?"

"Mrs. Crow, is it?" She could hear the woman's fingers skittering across her keyboard. "Yes... we had a call to pick up your husband, but when the tow driver showed up, no one was there. We assumed he was able to get on the road again. People always forget to call and cancel when that happens."

"But... you gave him a spare, right?"

"No ma'am, we didn't deliver a spare tire."

Rebecca froze. If it wasn't AAA, who was the man

in the van?

"Mrs. Crow, are you there?"

"Yeah... uh... I'm here. But, what do you mean, they couldn't find him? Did you go to the bridge? He said he saw y'all pull up in a van."

"Yes ma'am, we went to the bridge, but your husband wasn't there. And we don't show up with vans. All of our drivers are in tow trucks, for obvious reasons."

She reminded herself to breathe. They had to be somewhere safe. Oliver was with Jon who would move heaven and earth to make sure he was safe. But that didn't explain where Jon was... or why they hadn't called. Or why they weren't there when AAA showed up.

Or who was in that van.

"Mrs. Crow? I'm hanging up now. Have a good day and please remember to call us if you need help again in the future."

She stared at the phone's blank screen, unsure when the woman had hung up. The police: they would know what to do. Rebecca dialed 911 then hung up before it could ring. Was she over-reacting? Would they laugh at her and tell her to be patient? Was she supposed to wait twenty-four or forty-eight or whatever hours before calling them? They were okay. They would walk through the door any minute with a bag of burgers. They'd sit around the table and laugh about their adventure while eating and everything would be fine. Still, it was odd.

She dialed 911 again, and told herself everything would be okay.

3

Rebecca was still staring at the silent phone in her hand when red and blue flashing lights beamed across her front window, breaking the trance. She rushed to the door and yanked it open.

Standing on her front porch was a tall, broad-shouldered man with a kind face and a thick black mustache. He wore black slacks and a thin striped blue and white button-up shirt. A badge hung around his neck on a chain. In another life, Rebecca would have found him attractive. In another life, she wouldn't be standing there wondering where her husband and son were.

She peered around him to the white unmarked police cruiser parked in front of her house, to the left of her car. Jon's spot. Past the driveway, the street yawned empty on either side. If she stared hard enough, she could almost see Jon's blue Chevy pull up to the intersection, take a left onto their road, and cruise towards her. Oliver would be in the back seat, waving from the open window. They would park behind her car, and an avalanche of sandy feet, toys, and towels would spill out onto the concrete. Jon would say she was being silly, for calling the police. He would say she was being impatient, that she needed to relax. He always said she needed to relax.

Rebecca didn't dare look at the detective standing in front of her, because then it would be real. He would be there, and Jon and Oliver wouldn't. The minute that man came into her home and sat down on her couch clicking his pen and taking notes about the last time she saw or talked to her husband, it would be real. And she wasn't sure if she could handle that.

The detective reached out to touch her arm. "Mrs. Crow, did you hear me?"

She blinked and turned to face him.

"Mrs. Crow, I'm Detective Barnes with the Galveston County Sheriff's Office. You called us about a missing person?"

"Yes."

She took a deep breath, forced her shoulders back, and walked into the living room behind the detective.

The evening was a haze of strangers and coffee as other officers trickled in to assist, though most of them avoided making eye contact with her. Like a gossamer curtain, the potential contagion of her tragedy encircled her, trailing each uncertain step. Their downcast eyes and shuffled feet skirted around it, careful not to touch.

Modestly decorated, a brown fabric full-sized couch consumed the small living room. In front of the couch sat a coffee table, its glass surface marred by scratches. A pre-Oliver purchase, it hadn't been the same since he was old enough to bang his toys on it. A TV sat on a light wooden entertainment center against one wall, the screen blank. Rebecca and the detective sat on the couch with small blue pillows against their backs and cups of steaming coffee and tea on the table in front of them.

Detective Barnes pulled out his pen and pad of paper, and took notes as she walked him through her day. She was almost embarrassed at how little she remembered of their parting that morning, in too much of a hurry to get started on her work. Her work. It was all she had focused on the last few years before having Oliver. When their efforts to conceive took longer than they expected, the hyper-focus on her career was a welcome distraction. But even after he was born, it was the only place where she felt confident in what she was doing. And she was great at it. Even better at it than being a mom or wife. Rebecca racked her brain to come up with any details from that morning.

"Sammy."

The detective looked up from his notepad, one eyebrow raised in confusion, pen poised.

"His stuffed elephant, Sammy. That was... is... with him. It's this big..." She held up her hands about a foot apart. "And blue. He takes it everywhere. Is that important for you to know?"

"Sure." he nodded as he added it to his notes, "Anything else you can remember?"

She sighed. "No, I don't think so."

Barnes put his pen down and looked at her, his eyes searching her face.

"Mrs. Crow, is there anyone we can call? Anyone that can come be with you?"

She stared at her hands, rolled her wedding band around on her finger, and tried to think of who she could call. There was no one. Well, that wasn't completely true. There was her dad. But he was up in San Antonio, with stepmother number three. She could count on one hand the number of times they had seen each other since Rebecca had escaped her childhood home and never looked back. Before, it was just her and her dad, coexisting in silence and grief. Her mother's slow death from cancer put a strain on Rebecca's relationship with her father that was only improved by her absence. She thought it was because she looked so much like her mom, and she could understand that. Some days she got a glimpse of herself in the mirror and thought she was seeing a ghost. Especially as the years went by, and the wrinkles and weariness crept in.

When Detective Barnes touched her hand, her breath caught in her throat at the pity in his hazel eyes.

She lifted her chin and met his gaze, "No. Just find

Oliver and Jon... please."

"Ma'am, we'll do everything in our power to do just that, I promise. Do you have any pictures? As recent as possible, if you got 'em."

Of course Rebecca had pictures. She had hundreds of pictures, thousands of pictures. She lifted herself from the couch, feeling decades older than her thirty-five years should have felt, and went into the study to find their photo album. Returning, she placed it gently on the coffee table, careful to avoid the mugs of cooling tea and coffee. Her hands rested heavy on the cover as if the images of Jon and Oliver were the only things she had left of them. But they weren't. The detective would find them, and everything would be fine.

Unless it wasn't...

She opened the album and lifted each page with trembling fingertips, searching for the right picture. There was her and Jon's wedding; a small affair with only the two of them and about twenty coworkers and cousins. Dressed in the requested white and khaki attire, the guests sat on wooden folding chairs facing the water. The loose sand on the beach made for an uneven surface, and the guests had laughed about the sinking and shifting chair legs. A small arch of baby's breath and ivy kept watch over Jon and Rebecca's clasped hands. They had both changed so much, had become such different people from the happy, beaming couple that stared back at her from the pages of the album. She turned the page to find birthday parties and vacations when it was still only the two of them. Sipping pina coladas on exotic shores, snow skiing in Colorado, and the much begged-for trip to New York for Rebecca's 31st birthday. Next, there were maternity pictures taken by a friend of hers from college. Rebecca could barely remember her name... Veronica something. They sort of stayed in touch through social media since their days at the University. Mostly just liking each other's posts, never meeting in person for coffee or a movie or anything like that. In the pictures, Rebecca was standing on a bridge. Her downcast eyes focused on her swollen belly, and a hint of a smile peeked out.

Rebecca's hand went to her stomach, and she paused, the pages left open to those distant images of her. It had been a hard pregnancy. She was sick for most of it and had lost a lot more weight than their doctor was comfortable with. She could see it then, looking back at the pictures. Her cheek bones were more pronounced, and her green eyes were dark, covered in shadow. A weariness showed through the smiles. But it had all been worth it. As she kept turning the pages, there was Oliver. A tiny little thing swaddled with blankets and sleeping in the hospital bassinet. He was perfect. In the next photo, Jon held him close to his chest. He grinned ear to ear, beaming with pride. It seemed they had taken pictures of Oliver every day those first few years.

Then the photos showed Jon and Oliver at various parks, holidays, and the zoo. She remembered asking a stranger at the zoo to take one with all three of them in it, so there was one with her. Just the one. Otherwise it was all Jon and Oliver. That's the downside of being the amateur photographer in the family, she supposed. She was always behind the camera instead of in front of it.

As she flipped the pages, a slow movie unfolded. Similar to the flip books you made in class when you were younger, except instead of a pencil-drawn horse running, it was their life. Jon stopped appearing in them as much, as their arguments behind the scenes increased. She stopped joining them on their outings, as work demanded more of her time. Towards the end of the album, scattered shots of Oliver alone stared out at her from the pages. She hadn't realized how absent she had become until it was all laid out in front of her on the glass coffee table.

There he was at his first day of pre-school, so proud of his new lunch box. Jon had taken him because she had an important meeting at work that morning. When he printed the picture, Rebecca had hardly glanced at it before he shook his head and quietly placed it in the book. There on the couch with the detective, she lingered on the photo, caressing Oliver's face. She should have gone with them.

She shook her head and pulled her hand away. There was no use focusing on that. She couldn't change the past. But she couldn't use that picture, he didn't look like that anymore. His sandy hair was longer and parted to the side. She turned another page.

There was his first (and only) day of swim lessons. Oliver was standing at the edge of the indoor pool in his new bathing suit. They had made a big deal of shopping for the suit, in an effort to hype up the swimming experience. There was an empty smile plastered on his face, but it didn't fool anyone. His eyes were wide and worry lines wrinkled his forehead. They ended up leaving early, with Rebecca holding a shaking, soggy Oliver wrapped up in his old beach towel. She knew they should have started him in the 'Baby and Me' classes when he was younger, but life got busy and the time got away from them. It was at Rebecca's insistence that they finally made the time. Living so close to the beach, with its tide pools and canals, and the river emptying into the Gulf, she needed to be able to relax knowing he wouldn't drown. They left that day promising to give it another try soon. On another day, an arbitrary day in the never-ending string of days they expected to have together. That was two weeks ago.

Other pictures showed Oliver at his most recent birthday party, where he had turned four. Jon had picked him up in a bear hug and Oliver giggled that he couldn't breathe. That was when Rebecca snapped the picture. Shortly after,

Jon had released a laughing Oliver who immediately ran to join his friends. Purple and blue balloons had bounced on the breeze, anchored by twine to various chairs and table legs. She and Jon had stayed up late the night before, blowing up so many balloons that they became light-headed. It was a brief glimpse of the life they knew in the pre-baby years. They would stay up late talking and were blindly in love with each other. He was...

Rebecca caught herself already thinking about him in the past tense and started to cry. What could have happened to them? Why wasn't he answering his phone? She sat on the sofa and stared at the pictures for what seemed like hours until she felt Barnes' hand on her arm. She looked up, tears threatening to spill out, and realized he was waiting for her to hand him the picture she was holding – Oliver sitting at a table behind his birthday cake, smiling directly at the camera. This was silly, she told herself. It's a picture, it isn't him. She wasn't letting go of Oliver by giving Barnes the picture. But that's exactly what it felt like. As she handed Detective Barnes the photo, a heaviness settled over her chest, suffocating her.

4

Rebecca stood up from the couch and headed towards the kitchen, away from Detective Barnes and the painful photo album splayed on the coffee table. Wiping the tears from her eyes, she looked around for something to do. Anything but sit in that other room for one more minute. The pity in their eyes was horrible, the judgment; worse. They probably thought she was a terrible mother. Hell, maybe she was, but she didn't need them looking at her like that. She needed them to find her family, to do their damn job.

They shouldn't still be in her home, anyway. She'd told them everything she knew, at least six times. They should be out there, looking for Jon and Oliver. How many times could she walk through her day, going over every detail of what they were wearing, where they were going, and what he said in the phone call?

As many as it took, she supposed, until she remembered some small nuance or background noise. She wished desperately that she could remember something else. Their last conversation had replayed so many times in her head, the constant and steady buzz consumed her.

It was all so unreal. It was a dream that she would wake from any minute, with Jon snoring beside her in that annoying way of his, and Oliver asking for pancakes. Going through another growth spurt, he ate everything in sight. He was never a picky eater, not like Beth's girl Kelly. Kelly somehow subsisted on only cheerios and hot dogs. "It's a phase," Beth had told her. "They all go through it." Not Oliver, not yet anyway. Not ever? Rebecca frowned, she had to stop thinking like that.

Any minute they would walk through the door and wonder what all the fuss was about. Oliver would have fallen asleep on the way home, so Jon would carry him inside. Sometimes she knew he faked being asleep. She did that herself when she was a child. There was something about your parents carrying you into the house that made you feel safe and loved.

Jon would then pull Oliver's flip-flops off, dusting the carpet with a fine layer of sand. He would lay Oliver down on his race car bed and pull the covers up to his chin. It was a new comforter, blue with red and white race cars on it. Oliver had picked it out just a month before when he decided he was too big for his old one, a ragged thing left over from his toddler days. Pale green and splattered with cartoon lions, elephants, and giraffes, it had put in its time and was ready to retire. Jon would then lean down and move Oliver's unkempt curls off his sun-freckled forehead, clearing a space for a good-night kiss. He would close the door to Oliver's bedroom and tiptoe to the couch where he would fall asleep with the TV on. Jon would leave the car and its contents for Rebecca to clean up, along with the trail of sand to Oliver's room. She would need to wash his sheets the next day. Surely there would be sand and dirt on them. She never understood why Jon couldn't give him a bath first, after those trips to the beach. After cleaning up their mess, Rebecca would retreat to her office to get a leg up on the next day's workload.

From the living room, a loud squawk pulled Rebecca from her thoughts and into the present. It wasn't the sound that kept her attention; the thing had gone off intermittently all evening, but a drastic shift in the air. Serious and anxious to find her family all evening, the officers spoke as if their lungs had deflated. Unable to make out exactly what they were saying, she crept closer to the door to the kitchen. Fear kept her from running out to demand to be told what was going on, but she knew it wasn't good. She knew the minute the squawk of the radio sucked the hope out of the room. Unable to face whatever had happened, she stood frozen in the doorway, unnoticed by the officers gathering their things and heading towards the front door. Only Detective Barnes stayed behind.

He stood there for a minute with his back to Rebecca, still facing the closed front door. The departing officers' headlights swept back across the window as they pulled out of her driveway and headed down the street. Barnes' broad shoulders drooped, and his gaze stayed on the welcome mat in front of the door. He took a deep breath and turned around, not surprised to see her standing there.

"It could be nothing, ma'am, but some kids skinny dipping found a vehicle that matches the description of your husband's over in the canal. The officers are headed there now. It's probably nothing, vehicles get dumped there sometimes, but we have to go check it out. I'll call you as soon as I know anything."

Her chin quivered as she struggled to hold it up, "Where?"

Hesitation swept across his face as he answered, "The bridge, ma'am, over the canal."

A thousand questions beat at her throat while she wrestled to stay calm. After all, it was only a dream and everyone was safe, and she just needed to wake up.

She held his gaze and said, louder than she meant to, "Okay."

"Okay? Ma'am, are you sure there isn't anyone I can call to come be with you?"

"No, I'm fine. Let me know as soon as you hear anything, please."

He walked with her to the front door, asking again if

he could call anyone for her. Rebecca didn't like the sound of that at all. She didn't need him to call anyone because everything was fine. What she needed was for him to leave. She ushered him out and shut the door behind him.

She grabbed her purse and keys and peeked out from the front window, making sure his car was no longer in her driveway before slipping through the door and following him. She knew exactly where the bridge was. Rising high over the Intra-coastal Canal, it was hard to miss.

White knuckles gripped the wheel and her foot was steady on the gas. Stopping at every red light and using her blinkers at every turn, Rebecca tried to stay calm. Trying to convince herself that she wasn't in a hurry, that this was a normal trip down to the beach. She knew it wasn't, but pretending was so much easier than the alternative.

Rebecca was almost to the bridge when red and white beams pierced through the darkness ahead. They grew brighter as she pulled closer, illuminating a handful of officers, a tow truck, and other vehicles parked too far underneath the bridge to identify. She eased onto the side of the road, just beyond the circle of light. Her grip on the wheel tightened.

"Everything is fine, it's not his car, this is all just a mistake."

The intense weight of lingering summer heat hit her square in the chest as she left the coolness of the car, though the sun had long since set. The wind brought with it the smell of the sea and all its normalcy. It should smell different. It should smell like smoke, or rotten eggs, or anything else that would make more sense. But it didn't, it smelled like every other day at the beach. Except it was night, and she was walking towards flashing lights, hoping her life wasn't about to shatter into a million tiny pieces.

Rebecca saw the divers first. One was struggling to

remove his tank while the other, already tankless, sat on the tailgate of a truck. They didn't speak, their eyes staying fixed on the ground in front of them. They didn't even glance up as she ambled past, her own eyes locked on a group of officers near the edge of the water. Transfixed, she continued forward, relieved that the nightmare was finally starting to feel like one. Everything was hazy and there was quiet where there should have been chaos. Relieved, because it was so clearly something she would wake up from any minute, and her family would be safe…

"Hey! You can't be here!" A hand reached out and grabbed her elbow, fingernails digging into the soft flesh of her arm. Detective Barnes hurried over and released Rebecca from the grip of the young officer.

"What are you doing here?"

"Is it them? Is it his car?" she implored. Tears threatened, but she held them back with a few quick blinks and searched his face, hoping he would say no.

Before he could answer, the crowd of officers parted enough for her to see a car parked on the gravel. *His* car. Jon's blue Chevy, hooked up to a tow truck. The flashing lights of the patrol cars reflected in bursts on the glistening wet surface. She followed the trail of mud and water that led from the tires to the edge of the canal. Confused, she peered into the darkness that lay just out of reach of the light. Why weren't they smiling? Where were Jon and Oliver? If that was his car, they had to be there. They had been found. Everyone should be smiling.

She jerked away from the detective and ran towards the Chevy.

Rebecca was a few steps away from the car when she saw it. Through the open back door of Jon's Chevy, a small hand rested on the seat, its pale white skin a stark contrast to the dark interior of the car. A small hand, attached to a small arm, too still and bloated to be Oliver's. Ignoring the hands on her shoulders, she moved closer. It couldn't be her Oliver, her Oliver would never be that quiet. Her Oliver was safe and dry somewhere with Jon. This child was swollen and – her outstretched fingertips touched his hand – cold. Oliver's unruly blond curls stuck out at every angle, impossible to tame. This child's hair was darker, dripping water onto the brown seats. It couldn't be her Ollie. His eyes...

Detective Barnes tightened his grip on her shoulders and pulled Rebecca away from the car. Oliver's hand, lying there so innocent and so very cold, disappeared from her view as she collapsed onto the hard gravel. Rocks and dirt dug into her hands just before her world went dark.

5

Rebecca stood alone in a sea of black-draped mourners. The service was over and she was near Oliver's tiny white casket, numbly shaking hands while people shuffled by, their eyes averted. Funerals were always a bit easier when the deceased was old, or had a long-suffering disease. Those people were expected to die, to be put on display in front of everyone, to be lowered into the ground. Not children. You weren't supposed to bury children; everything about it was unnatural and horrific. No one knew what to say. Nothing could relieve the emptiness in her soul, the yearning to hold Oliver one more time, or to have Jon beside her, to lean on through the grief. She'd always been the strong and steady one of the two, but she didn't want to be that anymore. Couldn't be that ever again. She wanted to melt into the hard, white tile floor of the church and never get up. Oliver was a part of her. It wasn't fair, and no amount of bullshit platitudes of, 'well, he's in a better place,' or 'God needed another angel,' would change that.

Amy and Laura walked up to her with their pitiful faces drawn in, claiming to know what she was going through. Amy, as usual, wore a beautiful designer dress, solid black with delicate lace around her neck. The dark material contrasted with her pale white skin and striking black hair. Her small feet were tucked into modest heels, and she clutched a matching handbag to her side. Laura stood tall beside her, towering at least a foot over Amy. She was also wearing a long black dress, but you could bet she had purchased hers at Walmart, not at a designer store like her wife's. Laura never cared about things like that. They had buried their own child last spring, a daughter named

Alexandra who had been diagnosed with leukemia just the year before. Laura held Rebecca a little longer and patted her arm with a knowing smile, like she was now in the 'dead baby' club with them. Rebecca replied with the minimal amount of socially acceptable responses. A stiff hug, a murmured answer, and they were on their way. They couldn't know what she was going through, or what her baby had gone through. How could they? They could say goodbye to their child and hold her a little tighter, knowing it would be the last time. Alexandra had passed in her sleep, surrounded by people who loved her. People who had time to wrap their minds around what was happening and had each other to lean on. Oliver had drowned, scared and trapped in a car at the bottom of the canal. There was nothing they could say to bring her any ounce of comfort. She wasn't in a club. She wasn't burying her child, and she wasn't walking away from his small white casket to go back to a small empty house.

But she was.

She didn't even know if Jon was with Oliver at the end, or if he'd had to die alone, wondering where his mommy and daddy were. The people charged with keeping him safe had let him down. Jon was still missing, and Detective Barnes could only say that they were still working on it. But she knew, the longer it went on, the smaller the chance that they would ever find him. She was angry at Jon for allowing her baby to die, for not being there, and for making her bury their Ollie alone.

When the door closed behind the last mourner, Rebecca shuffled towards the front of the small white coffin. It was only a few feet from where she had been standing, but it felt like a mile. She was walking at the bottom of a pool and couldn't see past the surrounding haze. Every step was heavier than the last.

Rebecca placed her hands on the edge of the casket, one finger after another until her whole hand rested on the white satin that moved like water under her fingers. It was the purest white, the color of clouds on a bright sunny day, or cotton balls glued to a piece of construction paper. That was perfect for Ollie. White was the color of innocence, of a soul taken before life had tarnished it with its imperfections and suffering. And that was her Ollie – innocent. Not just innocent; he was pure. Loud, full of energy, and sometimes a lot to handle... but he could have everyone smiling within minutes of entering a room. To never see that smile again... she buried herself in self-loathing for not being there for him that day.

His face. She didn't want to look at his face, because then it would be over. She would have to say goodbye and they would close him up in that hard box, forever hiding his beautiful face. Still clutching the edge of the coffin, she glanced to her right. The setting sun danced through the stained-glass windows, casting shadows across the pews. The only other person left in the church was a stooped, gray-haired woman from the office. She was standing patiently by the front doors, waiting for Rebecca to leave so she could lock up.

Rebecca closed her eyes, turned her head, and lowered her chin towards her son.

There was another day, a much more joyful and bright day at the beach, just two months before. Oliver wanted them to close their eyes and try to find which way the sun faced by the warmth on their faces. Rebecca couldn't help but peek and had to stifle a giggle at the sight of Jon and Oliver turning in circles with their eyes closed. Eventually they all ended up facing the right direction and stood there for a minute, their cheeks flushed with warmth. He was her sun. But as she faced him with her eyes shut tight, his little body lying still on the cold satin, she couldn't feel him.

Somewhere, an air conditioner creaked to life and a cool breeze caressed her cheek. A bird tweeted a melody on the other side of the stained glass, and car doors slammed shut in the parking lot. She inhaled the scent of the arrangements of roses and tulips that surrounded her.

It was all wrong. Her Oliver smelled like dirt and gummy bears, not roses.

She took a deep breath and opened her eyes. His own blue ones were closed so sweetly, he could have been taking a nap. Her Oliver could never sit still for that long, even in his sleep. His golden hair was never that neat, but tousled from playing; a few sweaty strands stuck to his forehead. But the cold, neat little boy was her Oliver, she couldn't keep denying it.

There was the scratch on his cheek from trying to hug the neighbor's cat last week. Mrs. Ainsley had warned him about picking up Frank, the orange and white striped tabby. Frank was old and tried to avoid everyone. Ollie had snuck up on him while he was sleeping and put his arms around him. Frank was not pleased.

Tucked underneath Ollie's arm was his stuffed elephant, Sammy. Sammy was a lot better at receiving hugs than Frank had been. Rebecca had convinced Detective Barnes to let her have Sammy back and spent hours the night before washing the mud and salt water off of him. His mottled blue fur would never look like it did before, but it was important that Ollie have him close.

Ollie wore his favorite shirt, a white cotton T trimmed in blue. On the front was a lineup of sharks. Starting with a baby on the left, they grew larger as you went down the line, ending with a grandpa shark. She remembered the first day he had come home from Beth's house, singing that ridiculous song about baby sharks. It had driven her insane, but Jon loved it. He and Ollie ran around the house all week singing it. Below the shirt were his favorite khaki shorts. The ones with lots of pockets to put all of his treasures in. Around his neck was a red superman cape, the one he wanted to wear every day, but Rebecca would never let him.

She reached down and ran her fingertips through Oliver's hair, mussing it in the process. That was what his hair should look like. That was her Oliver... and he was gone. She would never again hear his sweet voice singing or his deep belly laugh. She wouldn't roll her eyes at the shark song or fight with him over a red cape. She would never again wipe sticky doorknobs or shake her head in frustration at his messes. She leaned over to kiss him and watched as a tear fell onto his pale round cheek.

Opening the door to the parking lot, the noise and brightness of living things assaulted Rebecca. In stark contrast to the quiet boy she had just left, a blazing sun beamed warmth onto her face. Leaves rustled in the breeze overhead, and somewhere in the distance a bicycle horn beeped. Life was still happening, just not to her. She was stuck in that dark, quiet place. Alone.

Her dad and his new wife, Paula, stepped away from the car hood they had been leaning on and walked towards her. He wore a suit that had seen better days. The elbows and knees were worn and the jacket hung open, unable to close over his ample belly. Paula had squeezed into a dress two sizes too small and, on heels three inches too high, tottered like a baby giraffe learning to walk. She appeared to be playing dress-up in someone else's clothes. Her long red hair hung straight, framing an oval face with entirely too much makeup. False eyelashes, heavy eye-shadow, and dark red lipstick created a faux clown look that had Rebecca shaking her head at the absurdity of it all. Her dad always did like them young and flashy. They had come down from San

Antonio for the funeral, though Rebecca wished they hadn't. She didn't need step-mother number three trying to relate to her over the body of her dead son. And this one was even younger than the last, almost Rebecca's age. She didn't need Paula or anyone else around who didn't love Oliver the way she and Jon had.

They helped Rebecca into the car and drove to her home. There wouldn't be a graveside service. Rebecca couldn't bear to see them lower her baby into the ground. She remembered her mother's casket descending into a dark hole, and the family throwing handfuls of dirt on top of it. It was a morbid tradition that she never understood. No, they wouldn't do that to her baby. The funeral parlor promised to handle him with care and she trusted them. After all, Ollie was gone. It was only his body they would be handling. It wasn't Oliver.

Her dad pulled his car close to the curb to let Rebecca and Paula out, then moved to park further down the street. Cars and trucks filled the driveway and lined the sidewalks, some of which Rebecca knew, others she didn't. She moved away from Paula's outstretched hand. She didn't need help to go into her own home. She wasn't fragile. She was Rebecca. Rebecca could handle anything thrown at her, not always with grace, but it would get handled. When she opened her front door, every head swiveled towards her while the remnants of dropped conversations hung awkwardly in the air. Great. Everyone look at the grieving mother. Scattered coughs and shuffles filled the room as people attempted to resuscitate their conversations.

She nodded politely at the few who were still looking at her, said "thank you" to a few others who mumbled condolences, and retreated into the kitchen. Leaning back on the counter, she watched the door swing back and forth on its hinges as it slowed and then stopped. She wasn't sure what she should be doing. Jon was the one with social skills. He would know exactly how to handle the crowd in their living room. The stoic, sympathetic mourners holding paper cups of sweet tea and snacking on veggie trays, careful not to spill anything on their nice clothing. But Jon wasn't there... so Rebecca hid out in the kitchen alone, hoping they would all just go away.

Casseroles, pies, jugs of sweet tea, cookies, and some pink fluffy dessert thing covered the counter behind her. That was the southern answer to everything: food. Lost your job? Eat. Boyfriend broke up with you? Eat. Husband missing and son dead? Eat. While appreciative of the thoughts, it only called attention to the fact that she was alone in the house, staring at enough food to feed an army. There was no way it would get eaten before it all spoiled, even if she had an appetite. How could she eat, or take any comfort in anything, when Oliver could never eat again, and Jon was – who knew where?

Every day that passed without finding Jon took them one step farther from ever finding him. She had watched enough crime TV shows to know if he didn't show up in the first few days, the chances were slim that he ever would. Jon's mother still didn't know about any of it. Her condition was 'delicate', and no one was sure how to handle her. Rebecca was the... well, the last living member of her immediate family if Jon was dead, and there were no cousins around to help with her.

Rebecca didn't have very much family left at all and – Alzheimer's or not – Claire was still her family. She should drive up to see her. The nursing home would be quiet; it seemed to be busiest on the weekends when children begrudgingly took time out of their schedules to put in their obligatory hour. Rebecca and Jon had made the trip a few times since Oliver was born, but it became harder to understand (or be understood by) her. Besides, with work and... *life*, it was hard to set aside time to spend on someone who wouldn't even know you were there. It was better for Jon, anyway. It was hard for him, seeing his mother like that. But at the moment, Rebecca welcomed the idea of sitting with someone who expected nothing from her.

Rebecca stayed in the kitchen for the majority of the evening, only reappearing to walk the last of the mourners to the door. Well, almost last. Her dad and Paula were still there. He picked up the trays and cups from the living room while his wife tried to arrange the Tetris game that was Rebecca's refrigerator. Both quietly worked, understanding that she didn't want to talk. Rebecca let them clean and sat down on the couch in the living room. She should have felt bad for resting while they worked around her, but she just didn't care.

As she sank into the old upholstery, she was glad for once they hadn't replaced it last summer when Oliver was eager to try out his new scissors. The scissors were child safe, but not couch safe. She moved the strategically placed pillow and touched the edges of the hole, wishing she hadn't yelled at him that day. It was a normal reaction. But then, sitting there on the couch alone, she wished she could go back and see his lips quivering and his blue eyes filling with tears and stop herself from getting angry. She wished she could have hugged him and told him it was Okay. But she couldn't. All she could do was sit there and feel the emptiness where he used to be.

The drapes near her were open – someone must have opened them – and a beautiful blue sky shone through the window. There wasn't a single cloud in sight. Two kids rode their bikes down the sidewalk, laughing to each other. The week before, Oliver rode on that same sidewalk. Jon had promised to take the training wheels off his bike that weekend. She winced at the realization of promises broken, and a future that would never come.

She jumped up, not noticing as the pillow dropped from her lap and hit the floor. She stomped towards the open window and gripped the edges of the plaid curtains. Laughter floated down the street as the kids turned the corner and disappeared. The hooks rattled on the rod as she jerked the curtains closed and remained facing them, fighting back a sob. It just wasn't fair.

At the sound of a throat clearing, she turned from the window to see her dad and Paula had entered the room. Had they watched her almost rip the curtains off the rod? Did she even care if they had? The kitchen was clean, and there was nothing left for them to do but leave.

"Honey, we can get a hotel and stay a few days, make sure you're okay," her dad said as he hugged her. His pale blue eyes glistened behind his thick glasses.

"I'm okay, really. I'm sure they'll find Jon any day now," Rebecca answered.

"Well, if you change your mind, please call me."

After she promised him she would, they walked towards the door and she thanked them for helping out. When they stepped onto the front porch, Paula turned to Rebecca.

"Honey, please don't hesitate to call if you need any-…"

Ignoring her, Rebecca closed the door of her house behind them and locked it, thankful for quiet at last. She returned to her spot on the couch, set her hand on the ragged edges of the hole in the fabric, and faced the closed drapes. She could shut out the bright sunny day, and the vision of children living and laughing, but she couldn't shut out the noises. Through the drapes and through the window, laughter echoed back at her. The kids must have turned around and headed back down her street. One of them called out something unintelligible to the other one, and they both laughed. The empty, dark house around her was so still and quiet. She could hear cars going down the street, dogs barking, and the click-click of her air conditioner as it struggled to keep up with the heat.

Life went on, but she couldn't. She didn't know how to exist in a world where Oliver didn't. She closed her eyes and leaned back, welcoming the flood of tears and sobs that drowned out everything else.

6

James' mama had lived in the Third Ward since as long as he could remember. About thirty minutes south of Houston, to him it was just the ghetto, where dreams came to die and the rent was always late. He blew that joint as soon as he could and hadn't looked back since, except to come see his mama from time to time.

The Third was an old neighborhood, one of the original in their shitty little town. Built with promise, every building had been new and full of hope. Back then, it was the place to be. But that was before they routed the highway over to the other side of town. Businesses in the Third took a big hit. No one wanted to drive across town for a haircut, or to use the laundromat anymore. Not with all the new places setting up shop over by the new highway. Thirty years later, they were left with a few crumbling churches held together by prayers and duct tape. The laundromat was still going, and the barber had his loyal customers, but relying on anyone living in the Third to keep you in business was risky. Most of them lived in homes they inherited or rented from slumlords. Either way, the houses were dilapidated. Broken shutters hung at odd angles, mold crept over faded paint, and cracks filled every sidewalk. It was the neighborhood everyone forgot. The city claimed to never have money to fix it up, and the Thirders couldn't afford to do it on their own. So, they just existed, day to day and as best as they could. It was a hard life. Most were uneducated and, if they had a job, underpaid. Others lived on government checks and child support. But they lived. To them it was home and the only community they had ever known. The Baptist church held dinners about once a month, and invited everyone even if they never had a butt in their pews. The Barber, Miles, would hook you up if you needed to look nice for a job interview but couldn't pay him. Thirders were good people.

James' mama's house was wood-framed and painted a bright yellow... about twenty years ago. Rusty metal pillars held up a small front porch, where she spent most of her days watching the neighborhood and being nosy. She was there, sitting on the front porch wearing nothing but an ankle length nightgown, when he pulled onto her gravel driveway. A faded fold-up lawn chair strained beneath her immense weight. Gray streaked through her dusty brown hair. She had once been beautiful; he knew. Not when she had ever been his mama, but before that. Before she met his dad and all the light was sucked out of her, leaving dull blue eyes straining to see the good in the world through her old metal glasses. When she saw him, she took a quick drag off her Pall Mall before twisting it out into the ashtray that balanced precariously on top of the mesh cup holder attached to the arm of the chair. A grin flashed across her face and her eyes lit up. Yeah, she used to be the kind of girl that would turn heads when she walked down the street. But that was about thirty years and three hundred pounds ago.

"Jimbo!"

She was the only one who could get away with calling him that. He'd knocked teeth out of guys twice his size for calling him that.

"Hey mama."

"Help me get up, now. I can do it, of course, but since you're here you don't mind helpin' your mama now, do you?"

She rocked back and forth while James held her arm to steady her, his fingertips disappearing into the creases and folds of her plump skin. Finally gaining the momentum she needed to project herself into a vertical position, she straightened with a huff; her cheeks red from the exertion. He put his arms around her and she hugged his neck before giving him a once over.

"Are you eating right? You look skinny. Come on in and let me cook you somethin'."

He wasn't hungry at all. In fact, he had just finished up lunch with Tommy at Captain D's, but he knew better than to deny her. He took a deep breath in, hoping he would have room in his stomach for more food.

"Sure mama, whatcha got?"

The screen door banged shut behind them as they went into the house. She moved like molasses, heaving from one foot to another, as she headed towards the kitchen.

"I tell you, Jimbo, that jackass Martin's got it in for me... sit down right there." She pointed to the only chair in the kitchen that hadn't yet buckled under her weight.

James sat and pulled his cigarettes out, tapping the pack on his palm before pulling one out and holding it up to her, eyebrows raised.

"Yeah, sure, but I'm gonna quit next week. Not today, Martin's got me needin' a smoke today."

She stuck it between her pale pink lips and leaned towards his outstretched lighter.

"Thanks," she mumbled around the cigarette before inhaling, bringing the small embers to life. "Anyway, I've only been late. What? Three times this year? And he wants to tell me I gotta pay him by the 15th or he's kicking me out! Well, I'd like to see him try, that little shrimp would blow over in a stiff wind. He can't make nobody do nothin', 'specially not Sandra 'goddamn' Porter. I wish a mother-fucker would. He'll get it when he gets it." She winked at James, "You want an egg sandwich?"

Without waiting for him to answer, she pulled a carton of eggs out of the old fridge and grabbed a skillet from underneath the counter.

"So his mama was tellin' everybody down at Tasha's Salon that he got himself a new woman and she's bleedin' him high and dry. Prancin' around town in those high heels and fancy dresses. Her dresses are so tight, she looks like a busted ass can of biscuits. What the hell does she need to get dressed up for? Looks like she's goin' to the damn prom." She chuckled. "Ain't no damn prom in the Third! Anyway, she's not workin' ever since she got caught stealin' from her boss. You remember Alfred down at the laundromat? So she was stealin' the coins down there so he fired her. Never got his money back, neither. Betsy was sayin' he only fired her 'cause she stopped sleepin' with him. He didn't mind her takin' the coins long as he could get some, but she stopped that when she started sleepin' with Martin."

James nodded along, smoking his cigarette. She popped two pieces of bread in the toaster and pulled out the sliced cheese and mayo from the fridge. The eggs slowly cooked as she stood in front of the skillet, spatula in one hand and cigarette in the other. She leaned on the counter for support and took a deep breath, her cheeks still pink.

"I tell ya, she must have some good stuff. She's got him all kinds of twisted up. His mama said she's tellin' him he's too nice, and he's gotta get tough and get his money when it's due, blah, blah. She don't care none 'bout his business, she just wants him to keep buyin' her stuff. You want one or two cheeses?"

James held up two fingers, and she unwrapped the cheese slices from their plastic covering. The toaster popped the bread up and she grabbed the hot slices and tossed them onto a paper plate, shaking her fingers to cool them off.

"So now he's all 'I need my money' and what am I supposed to do? *Shit* the money? I can't do nothin' 'till my social security check comes in and he knows that's not until the 1st!'"

She spread mayo on one slice of the toast and stacked the cheese on the other. Holding the cigarette in her mouth, she tipped the skillet over onto the cheese, scraping it down with the spatula. James watched as ashes fell into the eggs. She either didn't see it or didn't care. James figured the latter. Not that he really cared either. He'd been eating ashy food all his life.

"Now his mama, she's good people. She don't deserve a son like that, you know? He don't even call her no more, he's too busy layin' up with that hoe. Want a coke?"

She didn't wait for him to answer as she grabbed an orange soda from the fridge and popped it open, handing it to him.

She leaned against the counter again to catch her breath. "But I got this." She narrowed her eyes, "I see your face. That's your 'Imma handle it' face. But don't you worry none, Jimbo. Your mama been around for a long time and I didn't get this way by lettin' people take advantage of me. No sir, I learned that lesson a long time ago. You've done enough for your mama. I got this one, you hear? Martin can just kiss my big white ass. How's the sandwich?"

James nodded his approval, mouth full of toast and eggs. He wiped mayo off his chin and swallowed.

"It's good mama, thanks."

"I can make you another if you want."

"No, I'm good. Really, it's delicious, but this is enough."

"Why don't you like it? Did I put too much mayo?"

"Mom, it's good. I just don't want another one."

"See now you used to always want two sandwiches back when you weren't so damn skinny. It's probably the mayo, I had to buy it on clearance, but they said it was still good. You know those 'use by' dates are just suggestions.

They're good a long time after."

"It's not the mayo." James decided he needed to change the subject before she started cooking more eggs. "You doin' all right? With money, I mean?"

She waved her hand in front of her face, "Oh sure, don't you worry 'bout me."

"Seriously. I got a few jobs coming up and I can help out. How 'bout I take you down to the grocery store this weekend and help you pick some stuff out?"

"Jimbo I ain't never needed help pickin' stuff out, where the hell do you get shit like that?" She laughed and leaned back against the counter, wheezing.

"I'm just saying, I can help out, mama."

"I thought you said you wasn't workin' down at the shop with Tommy no more. Boy, you're havin' your own problems without worryin' 'bout mine."

James finished chewing another bite and took a swig of the orange soda, trying to think of how much to tell her. "I got somethin' new comin' up, it pays real good."

"I'm proud of you, baby. You goin' to the plants finally? I been tellin' you for years you gotta go to the plants for the real money."

He finished his sandwich and stood up to take his plate to the trash. "Screw the plants, that's just a bunch of yes-men bending over every day. No lube, neither. No, this is something else, something me and Tommy been working on. Sit down, mama, you're gonna have a heart attack."

The chair legs groaned under her weight as she plopped down. Beads of sweat glistened on her pale forehead.

"Oh, I like that Tommy, you need to bring him 'round more. Tommy's good people. He'll steer you right, he don't do drugs or nothin'."

"Yeah, Tommy's all right. So anyway, I gotta go

mama. I was just checkin' in on ya. You sure I can't handle this Martin business? I don't mind talking to him."

"Okay, my shows fixin' to come on, anyway. And no, don't you worry about Martin. I told you I got this." Her smile faded as she held his gaze, "Don't go doin' nothin' stupid now. You done did enough for one lifetime, you need to stop tryin' to take care of me."

"Fine, I'll leave it be." He wouldn't, of course, but that's what she wanted to hear.

He washed his hands, hoped the churning in his stomach wasn't the expired mayo, and wrapped his arms around her sides as far as they could go. As he leaned in to kiss her on the cheek, he breathed in the cheap perfume, mosquito spray, and cigarette smell that had always surrounded his mama.

She stood on the front porch, waving to him as he pulled out of the driveway and onto Ave J. He took a left on Eleventh St. and headed out of the Third Ward. He'd take care of things. Hell, he'd been taking care of her since he was ten, he wasn't about to stop now. That Martin wasn't nothing he couldn't handle.

7

James was ten when he killed his father.

It was a school day, an otherwise normal day filled with otherwise normal happenings. James was waiting for his mama to pick him up in front of his school, surrounded by a crowd of otherwise normal children. Since he was bringing home his science fair project, she offered to give him a ride instead of his usual spot on the bus. The styrofoam solar system balanced on his knees as he sat on the curb and waited for her. He watched the buses pull away from the lot, filled to the brim with tired school children. The stragglers had been picked up and teachers were walking to their cars when he realized she wasn't going to come get him. James gathered his things and set off on foot towards home.

Four miles wasn't a terribly long walk for a ten-year-old, but the project was awkward to balance and try to see around. As he continued on, he stumbled over cracks in the sidewalk, his vision blocked by a bouncing red ball labeled 'Mars'.

He was two houses away when the first scream pierced the late afternoon air. Hours of hard work hit the ground with a clatter as thin metal rods fell to the sidewalk and planets rolled into the ditch. James was at his front door in seconds. Inside, his mama was on their kitchen floor surrounded by amber colored pieces of glass and a dark sticky liquid. Her long brown hair hung limply, obscuring her face. She wiped a cut on her mouth with the edge of a yellow kitchen towel embroidered with 'Bless This Kitchen'. Red streaks snaked among the green letters. She lifted her chin and her bloodshot brown eyes widened when she saw James. She gestured frantically for him to go to his room and stay quiet, but for the first time in his life, James didn't listen to her.

"James, go!" she cried out as quietly as she could.

But he stayed there, feet frozen to the chipped linoleum. He didn't want to run and hide, wondering when it would be his turn. He was tired of the routine. If his dad was going to beat on him anyway, at least he could offer himself up now and hopefully take the attention off his mama for a little bit.

"Boy, didn't you hear your mama? Go to your goddamn room!"

His dad stood in the doorway to their living room, bent over slightly so his head didn't bump against the wooden frame. Steel brown eyes – so dark they were almost black – glared at James. He was still in his work clothes, dark blue pants and a matching button-up shirt. An electrician at one of the big chemical plants, he was usually still at work when James got home from school. They must have had more layoffs; that was the only reason he ever came home early. There had been rumors for weeks but until then, his dad had been able to avoid the cuts.

James raised his chin defiantly and his small voice trembled as he whispered, "No."

His dad was on him like white on rice, wrapping calloused hands around James' throat before he could regret his reply. James struggled for breath, clawing at his dad's fingers as his mama screamed and tried to pull him away. No one said no to Gary Porter. Eyes bulging with rage, whiskey scented spittle flew from his mouth. This was it, James thought. This is how he was going to die. He stopped fighting back and looked his dad in the eye. For a minute, he was relieved. Death meant that he wouldn't have to take his math test in the morning. That Mrs. Thompson could be a real bitch. She had it in for him; he knew it.

Disgusted, his dad shoved James into the side of the fridge. It wasn't as fun if he didn't fight back. "Get me a beer," he growled. "Your mama forgot to buy more whiskey so now I gotta drink that piss."

His mama dropped back to her knees to clean up the mess on the floor, her hands shaking and her tears mixing with the glass shards and spilled whiskey. Blood soaked through the knees of her jeans, and more had dripped down onto her T-shirt from the cut on her mouth. She was smaller back then, just a normal-sized mama putting up with an asshole-sized dad. Frustrated, James opened the fridge and yanked a bottle of beer out. Stepping over pieces of the broken bottle, he made his way to the drawer by the microwave. That's where his dad liked to keep the bottle opener so he could pop a few while waiting for his dinner to heat up. It didn't matter if he had whiskey or not, Gary Porter always found a reason to chug a PBR, or five. James tip-toed to the living room. His dad didn't like a lot of noise when he got that way, which was more often than not.

James was sick of it. Sick of worrying about her, sick of tip-toeing around his dad's moods, and most of all sick of his asshole dad. He didn't look up from the TV when James held out the bottle. He just reached for it and took a big long swig. He wiped his mouth on his sleeve and slammed the bottle down onto the end table next to him. He would never stop, James realized. Not until he killed his mama or him, anyway. Not even then, James supposed. He would find someone else to marry and beat on before grass started growing back over their graves. That was just who Gary Porter was, who he would always be.

When James walked back through the kitchen, his mama was leaning against the counter, holding the stained yellow towel and looking wistfully out of the window over the sink. James leaned forward to see what she was looking at, but it was just their front yard. Nothing special or different about it. The same yard that needed mowing, the same sidewalk with grass growing up between the cracks, and the same old cars parked there. The mailbox hung at an angle ever since someone hit it with a baseball bat a few months before.

"Mama, you okay?"

She didn't turn around as she answered, her voice shaking, "Yeah, baby. I'm fine. I'm sorry I wasn't able to get you from school. You know how he gets when he's laid off... how'd the teacher like your project?"

"I got a ninety-five, it was one of the best ones," he beamed, before realizing all of his hard work lay smashed on the sidewalk outside where he had dropped it.

"That's good, baby. I'm proud of you." She continued staring out of the window.

One year, when he had turned five, his dad had given him a pool float for his birthday. It was magnificent, an almost life-sized great white with a big grin on its face. His dad had howled with laughter at the confusion on James' face. Having spent all summer asking for one of those big above-ground pools, James couldn't understand why his dad would give him this when his answer was always an angry 'no'. Maybe he had changed his mind, James hoped, looking up at him with excitement. His dad helped him blow it up with his rusty bicycle pump and James had stood next to him, excited at what it might mean. Maybe they had gotten him that pool after all. That was the moment Gary Porter took out his pocket knife and stabbed the shark just under the fin. Dragging his knife along its side he looked at James through narrowed eyes, "now will you stop asking for a goddamn pool?"

James never forgot that day, or how his shark looked crumpled up on the ground with all the air out of it. That's how his mama looked right then, leaning against the sink. Deflated. Ten years of anger welled up inside James. He ran to his parent's bedroom before he could change his mind.

He knew where his dad kept his gun, the Beretta M9 he had shown James how to shoot on a rare afternoon of father and son bonding in the field behind the Quick Mart. James spent most of that day worried his dad would shoot *him*, but he didn't, so it was a pretty decent afternoon overall.

The gun stayed loaded. His dad liked to stay prepared for anything.

"I bet he didn't prepare for this."

He tucked the gun into the waistband of his jeans and covered it with his shirt. Afraid it would slip down the inside of his pants, he carefully shuffled back through the kitchen towards the living room. His mama was still standing at the sink, staring blankly at the blood-soaked towel. James took a deep breath and quickened his step. He should have done this months (years?) ago. His dad, hearing him come into the living room, yelled at him to get another beer, not taking his eyes off the television set.

"Okay."

James tiptoed closer until he stood behind the overstuffed recliner. He pulled the gun out of his waistband and raised it to the back of his dad's head. He thought back to that day in the field. Arms stiff but elbows slightly bent. Right hand holding the gun, left hand cupping the bottom of his right firmly. Safety off. He pressed the tip of his index finger on the trigger, but it was harder to pull than he remembered. He took a deep breath and moved his finger to get a better grip.

Bits of dandruff floated among the dirty blond hairs at the back of his dad's head.

His mom sniffled in the kitchen.

James squeezed the trigger.

A deafening boom filled the small living room, and the gun kicked up and over James' head. His sweaty hands struggled to keep hold of it while the ringing in his ears deafened him. His mama ran into the living room, eyes darting around frantically as she took in the macabre scene. Staring at what used to be the back of his dad's head, James still stood behind the patched tan recliner. There was only a tangled mess of blood, hair, and what looked like brains. James had never seen a brain before, and it was nothing like he had imagined. But he had imagined a brain fully intact and his dad's... wasn't. His dad's brain was all over the front of the TV, even on the empty bottle of beer sitting on the table. James wondered if he had known it would be his last bottle, would he have savored it more? Probably not. His dad wasn't exactly the 'savoring' type.

With the gun still in his hands, he felt like he could take on the entire world. He was proud to have finally stood up to his dad and protected his mama. The corners of his mouth hinted at a smile as he tore his gaze from the blood and hair draped beer bottle and looked up at her, his eyes wide. She was staring at him with a blank expression on her face.

She carefully took the gun from his shaking hands.

"Don't say a word. Wash your hands, real good, not like you normally do. Then, go to your room. You've been there all evenin' and only came out when you heard a gun go off... understand?"

"James, do you understand?"

He nodded and walked to the kitchen. His ears were still ringing and he couldn't get his right hand to stop quivering. He stood close to the door and tried to listen as his mama called 911.

After telling them her name and address, she coolly said, "I just shot my husband, please come quickly."

James knew they would arrive fast, they usually did when the neighbors called, hearing his mama's screams from their house next door. He scrubbed his hands in the sink and rushed to his room, wiping his wet hands on the legs of his jeans. He kicked his shoes off and laid down on his bed, wondering what he should do next. Noticing his book on the nightstand, James picked it up and settled down to read. He was only a few chapters in when there was a sharp rap on his door. He quickly put the book back on the nightstand and stood up. Would it be rude to lay there reading while his father was in the recliner missing the back part of his head? James didn't know, he was never good at knowing what was rude. His mama was constantly telling him, "James you can't say things like that," or, "James be nice." Nice was so confusing, but he loved her, and she had so few pleasures in their miserable life, so he tried. For her.

He was halfway to the door when it opened from the other side and a somber-faced policeman stepped into his room. It was Williams. He had stayed with James a few times before, when the cops had to come talk to his parents. He answered the questions as politely as he knew how, and just like his mama said to, before Williams closed his notebook and stuck it back in his pocket.

"Can I go see my mama now?"

The officer tilted his head, "Of course son, no one said you couldn't."

His mama had convinced them she was protecting James. With the hand marks on his throat, her injuries from being knocked to the floor, and their history, it was believable. If they had doubts, they didn't show it. They all looked relieved that their days of rushing to the Porter house were over. No more time wasted interviewing a beaten woman who kept refusing to press charges.

He stood by his mama on the front porch as the

ambulance that carried his dad's body pulled out of their driveway and headed down the road. Years of tension and stress rode with it. James reached out and held his mom's hand.

He supposed there would be a funeral, and they would have to pretend to be sad. That was fine. As long as his dad was gone, James could do anything.

8

Rebecca drove to San Antonio the next day, pulling into the nursing home's parking lot a little after noon. She sat in the car with the engine running and reconsidered her trip for at least the tenth time that morning. Claire was in the advanced stages of Alzheimer's and, depending on the day, might know who Rebecca was, understand what she was telling her, and have her heart broken; or not remember who she was, and it would be a wasted trip. She should have just stayed home. Home. An empty building with nothing but echoes of life that threatened to consume her. She was glad at least to be out of that place, even if turned out that she wouldn't be able to talk to Claire.

She angled the rear-view mirror down to check her makeup and glimpsed the booster chair secured to the middle seat. Her hand froze on the edge of the mirror. Oliver was sitting there, kicking his heels against the hard plastic booster and waving to her. The grin on his sweet face crinkled to the edges of his big blue eyes, and wayward strands of curly blond hair tickled the tops of his eyelashes. He tilted his head to the side to see around his hair, still smiling. His small, not pale arms reached out to her with grasping fingers.

Gulping, Rebecca didn't dare move. She wasn't sure why Oliver was in her backseat, but she was glad for it. Tears rolled down her face as she held her breath and stared at him in the mirror. Unable to resist any longer, she turned away from the mirror to face the backseat. There was his booster, snugly secured to the middle seat.

Empty.

She wiped her tears away and shook her head.

The car door opened with a click and she stepped out into the parking lot. The black asphalt crunched beneath her feet while she made her way to the sidewalk. It had been over six months since they were there last. That trip had been harder than most; they were all crying by the time they poured themselves back into the car. Even Oliver, who hadn't been sure *what* he was crying about. Claire had been more alert than usual, angry even. They were trying to enjoy the nice weather on the back patio, but Claire wanted Jon to take her back to her home. Jon gently reminded her – again – that she no longer had a house; they had sold it to help pay for the nursing home. She tried to walk to the parking lot to get in Jon's car and the nurses had to force her back into her room. Confusion only fueled her anger. Yelling at Jon and Rebecca to help her, they had to look her in her eyes as they shook their heads. The only thing they could do to help at that moment was leave. Their presence obviously made her situation worse. The visits weren't always like that, but it made it hard to want to go back. Jon said they should stay away for his mother, so she wouldn't be as confused by her old life walking into her new one. Rebecca agreed, but for her it was so she, Jon, and Oliver wouldn't have to witness another episode like that.

Selfishly, she was glad they no longer went to visit Claire. Nursing homes had always given her the creeps, with their death smells and vacant-eyed patrons. It was too clear a reminder that no matter how hard one fought it, age crept up and consumed everyone.

But Claire, the Claire before the Alzheimer's claimed her, loved Jon and Oliver almost as much as Rebecca did. She was Rebecca's last connection to them, the only person left in the world who would truly know her pain – on a good day, anyway. She shook her head and frowned as she made her way down the sidewalk. She knew it was selfish, wishing a good day for Claire's mental faculties so Rebecca could break her heart, but she needed someone to mourn with her. Someone who knew.

The bell over the door tinkled when Rebecca pushed it open and stepped into the foyer. An umbrella and coat stand, empty but for a single forgotten yellow umbrella, stood to her right. Past the front desk to the left of the entrance was a sitting area, three long couches with soft pillows and worn blankets draped over the backs of each. In the corner waited a small basket of toys for younger children to occupy themselves with. It was the visiting area people used if the weather outside was bad or they just preferred to sit indoors. The antiseptic mustiness of it all enveloped Rebecca immediately. A small woman sat at the front desk. Her long hair, dark brown except for about an inch and a half of gray roots, cascaded down her shoulders. She furiously typed away at her computer, oblivious to the sound of the bell over the door. Startled, her head jerked up when Rebecca said hello.

"Well my goodness, if it isn't Mrs. Crow! You scared the daylights outta me. How are ya, hon?" She looked around Rebecca to the door behind her, "Where's Jon and the little one?"

"Hi, they... um..." Rebecca hesitated before clearing her throat. "They couldn't make it today."

"Well, that's okay now, what a fine idea for you to come see her by yourself. She's having a much better day than that last time. Wasn't that just awful, poor Claire was just screaming and..." She stopped as she noticed Rebecca fidgeting, her skin pale. "Hon, are you all right? You don't look so good."

Coming around from behind the counter, she stepped closer, but Rebecca held up her hand, "I'm okay, really I am. It was just a long drive in, that's all. I'm going to run to the restroom before I see her."

Needing to get away from the woman, despite her well-intentioned sweet nature, Rebecca turned down her offer to walk her to the bathroom, insisting she remembered the way. That woman, with her unknowing cheerfulness or her pity, was the last thing Rebecca needed. She avoided looking at herself in the mirror as she washed her hands, afraid she would once again see an Oliver that wasn't really there. She knew she looked awful anyway; she didn't need a reminder. Dark circles had taken up permanent residence underneath her eyes, she had pimples for the first time in years, and had thrown on her clothes without care. At least she had showered, she thought, drying off her hands.

Leaving the restroom, she made her way towards Claire's room, careful to avoid being seen by the woman at the front desk. She passed mostly closed doors on her way down the hall, some with cheerful homemade signs, others left undecorated as the occupant had no family left, or at least none that visited enough to care about what their door looked like. A few doors were open just enough to let snippets of TV shows, radios, or the rare visitor chatter trickle out into the hallway. Some open doors revealed nothing but quiet and darkness, leaving Rebecca to wonder why they were open at all. Stepping around a corner, she saw the closed door to Claire's room. She stood before it with her knuckles raised to knock and paused, staring at the blank white surface of the door. It was possible Claire was taking a nap or reading, but she didn't want to interrupt the silence on the other side of the door. She lowered her hand and quietly turned the handle.

Claire was asleep in her bed, her time-ravaged face framed by thin, silver hair. Her closed eyelids twitched rapidly. Dreaming of better days, Rebecca hoped. Someone had drawn a patchwork quilt up beneath her chin, its colors and stitching faded with time. Jon's mom had been quite the quilter in her day, when she could still hold a needle steady and firm. A lace doily covered the wooden nightstand beside the bed on which sat a lamp, a pair of reading glasses, an emergency button on a string, and a single framed picture. The picture, like the frame, was timeworn. There were spots scattered around the wooden edge of the frame, made smooth over the years by caressing fingers. Inside, a picture of Claire and Tomas, Jon's dad. They were kneeling in the grass in the shade of a large oak tree, its branches heavy with Spanish moss. Jon, just a baby at the time, was sitting between them on a blanket, grinning that silly wondrous smile that babies do. Claire and Tomas were looking at him and beaming with pride. It was the perfect family, full of love.

Until it wasn't.

Shortly after that picnic beneath the tree, doctors diagnosed Tomas with colon cancer, stage four. Within a month, the illness had reduced the robust man smiling in the picture to a frail, thin man, with a gaunt face and hollow eyes. Claire had taken one last family picture of her and Jon sitting on the edge of his dad's hospital bed. That one didn't make the doily-covered nightstand. That one was tucked away in a box on a high shelf of Rebecca and Jon's closet. No one was smiling. The treatment had taken Jon's father from them before the cancer ever did. It was one thing they had bonded over on their first date, the understanding you only gain after watching someone you love suffer like that. Claire never recovered. He was the love of her life, and she had no desire to meet anyone else or take her time away from raising Jon. Rebecca touched the baby's cheek in the photograph and smiled. Claire had done an excellent job raising her son in a peaceful home full of love and affection; no one could ever doubt that.

She wiped the tear that had found its way down her cheek and looked around the room, unsure how to proceed. Rebecca knew if she turned around and left, she would lose the nerve to do what she came for, so she settled into the old chair next to the window and waited.

Claire had one of the best views in the building. About fifteen feet from the window, there was a sitting area with wooden benches surrounded by perfectly maintained shrubs, blue and yellow flowers planted with care in perfect rows, and tall oak trees whose leaves rustled with a light breeze. Like the tree in the picture on Claire's nightstand, they were also adorned with Spanish moss, gently waving as it cascaded down towards the grass. Beyond the trees, she could barely make out a wooden fence line. It was a fine balance, showing the beauty of the nearby forest but still needing to keep the elderly residents contained.

A stooped, elderly man shuffled alone towards the fence. Almost there, he stopped and stared out into the woods. What he was looking at, Rebecca couldn't tell. But he stood there, watching something while she watched him. Perhaps he had caught sight of a bird or a rabbit. Or, maybe he was thinking about his old life, past that fence. A life in which he would never again be an active participant. His shoulders seemed to sag a little more as he turned back towards the benches. Rebecca was still watching as he turned to face the woods again and carefully lowered himself down onto the bench. Old joints required a slower transition. Rebecca herself could feel the years settle in as she drew a foot underneath her and nestled further down into the chair, leaning her head back. A lone mosquito buzzed around the windowsill as she twirled her wedding ring around her finger and watched the back of the man's head. Wisps of thin gray strands peeked out from his threadbare tan fedora, contrasting with the chestnut skin at the back of his neck.

Jon had finally started to show gray, but it was contained to the area around his temples. In their earlier years, Rebecca had run her fingers through it as they talked about growing old together.

Rebecca's arms flailed as she awoke with a jerk. Exhausted, she had dozed off while waiting for Claire to wake up. Looking towards the bed, she watched as the old woman's chest moved up and down with every ragged breath. Relieved that she hadn't missed her waking up, she turned back towards the window. Outside, the man was still sitting on the bench but his head had fallen into a sharp angle. That couldn't be comfortable. A bird landed on his shoulder, and still he didn't move. Rebecca knew without knowing, that he was gone. It was such a peaceful way to go. Perhaps when he woke up that morning he knew it would be his final day. Maybe he dressed himself in those corduroy pants, tan loafers, and pearl snapped shirt knowing it would be the last time. Had he lived a good life?

What was a *good* life? Was it having people to love who loved you back? Was it doing good deeds? Was it righting the wrongs of others? Rebecca didn't know anymore. Her good life was becoming a distant memory. Now a good day meant getting dressed, eating a meal, the things most people could do easily.

She knew she needed to tell someone, the staff would need to collect his body and notify his family. They would mourn, as they should. But it wouldn't wreck them. Their lives wouldn't be completely torn apart. Nursing homes were, after all, transitional places as much as places of care. Sons and daughters adjusted to lives without their parents, grandchildren without their Paw-paw or Granny. So, when the news came, it was expected and everyone was ready. Still, Rebecca sat in the chair facing the window. He was peaceful, and they were blissfully ignorant. Maybe things should stay like that as long as they could.

She straightened her leg out in front of her, and hundreds of tiny pins pricked her foot as the blood rushed back into it. Rebecca massaged her foot and glanced again towards Claire's bed. She was still sleeping, her mouth open, spittle escaping and making its way towards her pillow. Rebecca stood and walked to the side of Claire's bed. She reached down and picked up her frail, wrinkled hand. The skin shifted under Rebecca's touch, threatening to slide off altogether.

She braced herself and whispered, "Mother, it's me, Rebecca. Can you wake up for a few minutes? Please wake up, I need to talk to you."

Claire didn't budge.

"Mother, mom..." Rebecca raised her voice and squeezed her hand. Still nothing. She glanced towards the door. Maybe an orderly would come in to give medicine or check on her and they could wake her up. But no one came.

She had to do it.

"Mom..." She leaned in closer to Claire's ear, "Mom. MOM!"

Claire coughed as her milky blue eyes slowly opened, filled with confusion. For a second, Rebecca worried she had come all that way for nothing, that Claire wouldn't remember her. She watched the memories trickle in behind her eyes while Claire wiped her mouth with the back of her hand, squeezed Rebecca's with the other, and smiled.

"Becky, honey, is that you?"

Relieved, Rebecca squeezed her hand. "Yes, mother. It's me."

Looking around the room, Claire asked in a weak, still sleepy voice, "Where's Jon and Ollie?"

Rebecca took a deep breath and carefully placed Claire's hand back on the edge of the bed. Dragging the chair over to the side of the bed, she sat and picked Claire's hand back up, holding it in both of hers.

"They're gone..." Rebecca's eyes filled with tears. "Jon is missing and Oliver is... Oliver is…" She couldn't bring herself to say her Ollie was dead, cold and buried among dirt and pebbles. Claire's brow furrowed and her bottom lip began to quiver.

Louder this time, she asked, "Missing? What do you mean, Becky? And Ollie is what?"

Rebecca took a deep breath and proceeded to tell her mother-in-law everything that had happened in the last week. The frail woman's once twinkling blue eyes filled with despair. Tears coursed their way down the deep lines on her face, but she didn't move to wipe them away.

Rebecca held Claire's hand as she cried, overcome with grief. She grabbed a tissue from the nightstand and wiped tears from Claire's face, wondering if she did the right thing in coming here. As she settled back down and the tears slowed, Claire looked at her, confused.

"Becky honey, is that you?"

Rebecca squeezed her hand again and said "Yes, mother. It's me."

Looking around the room, Claire again asked "Where's Jon and Ollie?"

Rebecca sighed, unsure how to proceed. "Remember mother, we just talked about it..."

Claire stared at her blankly.

Rebecca told her again what happened, or what the cops thought happened, and hoped it was the last time she would have to relive those moments. It wasn't. Rebecca recounted the horrible events a total of four times that day before she just couldn't any more.

"Becky honey, is that you?"

"Yes, mother. It's me."

"Where's Jon and Ollie?"

Rebecca stared into the hazy blue eyes. Her shoulders slumped as she answered, "They're just outside, mother. They'll be here in a minute."

"Oh okay, that's nice. Did you see they gave me new curtains?" Claire pointed to the window.

"Yes, they're beautiful." Rebecca leaned over, inhaling the stale aroma of dust and old sheets as she kissed Claire on the forehead.

Squeezing her hand one last time, she released it and said goodbye. Rebecca knew she wouldn't be returning. The one person who loved Jon and Oliver the way she had... was gone. Her presence didn't bring Claire comfort or peace, but confusion and grief.

Rebecca closed the door to the room with a soft click and walked out of the nursing home. She ignored the woman's greeting from the front desk, incapable of small talk or questions, and kept walking until the front door had shut behind her. As she stepped outside into the thick afternoon heat, her breath caught in her chest. She didn't make it halfway to the car before she dropped to the ground, sobbing. Hard asphalt dug through her jeans and scratched her knees. Hands splayed on the pavement of the sidewalk, she closed her eyes as tightly as she could, hoping to shut off the tears at the source. There was no one to share this with, to draw comfort from. Unless they found Jon soon, she didn't know if she could make it. She didn't know if she wanted to.

9

———

The cop's unmarked Ford Crown Vic was two blocks from James, weaving around parked cars and puttering down the street towards the house he shared with Tommy. James always could spot a uniform a mile away. Something in the way they drove, that quiet tip-toe down a street. Or, it could be that all the cops in their damn town drove Crown Vics.

It was a summer weekend, so the beach was overflowing into his neighborhood. Trucks, cars, and scooters lined the avenue around him, their owners abandoning the idea of finding a parking spot on the sand and just grabbing the first available curb they could find. He stood on his balcony, cigarette in one hand and coffee cup in the other, watching vehicles vomit families and beach gear all morning. He leaned on the railing and wondered if any of them had left their doors unlocked. Out of towners were usually easy pickings but there were too many of them around today to wiggle any door handles.

The car that was trying really hard not to look like a police car (but you knew it was from the tentative way it weaved around the cars and the long antennae sticking out from the roof) was almost to his house. James twisted his cigarette out on the railing and flicked it over the edge where it fell to the ground, joining the pile of previously discarded butts that lay scattered beneath the balcony. He slid the patio door open and went back into the living room, closing it shut behind him. That hadn't taken long. He was actually a little surprised at how quickly the cops had found him and Tommy. Tommy probably snitched to someone at work. The little shit couldn't keep a secret to save his life and he'd been all twisted up since that kid died.

James lit another cigarette and sat down on the faded blue couch. It would take the detective a minute to park, then a few more minutes to walk up the stairs to the front door. Theirs was one of many stilt houses on the beach. The porch view was great, and you could be in the water within five minutes of closing your front door behind you, but the place itself was falling apart.

When he and Tommy answered the ad, they expected to see what was promised... a cheap but decent two-bedroom, one bath beach house, fully furnished. It did have two bedrooms, and it did technically have one bathroom if you counted the small tiled nook upstairs and the outdoor shower downstairs. The shower did have four walls so there was privacy, but it was missing a roof and had a clumsily poured, uneven concrete floor to stand on. It was a dump. James didn't consider a chipped flea market coffee table, two wicker chairs that looked like they survived the flooding from Hurricane Ike, and a table in the kitchen that had to have a stack of sugar packets shoved underneath one leg to stay steady, to be 'furnished'. Still, it was cheaper than the others they had looked at that day and they needed a place fast. James had grown tired of living with his mama; it was putting a real dent in his time with the ladies, and Tommy had just caught his boyfriend Albert cheating on him. You'd think Tommy would have been the one to keep the house since he was innocent in the whole matter, but Albert's cousin owned the place so what could you do? Tommy was out on his ass. James was never one to let a friend go without if he could help, so he moved in with him. Not that he had really helped much with rent and bills since he got fired by that prick Trey, but he was going to as soon as he had some cash.

James heaved himself up from the couch and crossed

the living room into the kitchen. The whole place shook anytime you walked somewhere, so he knew the cop could tell someone was home. If he had parked already and started up the stairs, that is. James figured it was only a matter of time before the whole place came tumbling down. But until that happened, he and Tommy were gonna sit pretty and pay the rent until they could save up for something nicer. Or, he would sit pretty while Tommy paid the rent. James opened the fridge, sniffed the expired carton of milk, and chugged a few gulps before he placed it back on the shelf. He wiped milk dribble off his chin with his sleeve and hoped that would be enough to cover up the smell of alcohol he knew was on his breath. Not that there was a law against drinking in your own damn house at one in the afternoon, but he didn't want to give the detective any reason to take special notice of him. He did just kill a man after all, he and Tommy. Oh yeah, his little snot-nosed kid too. But James figured that didn't really count. They didn't actually kill the kid. They sure didn't stop the car from going into the water, even after they saw his face pop up in that back window, but they didn't fucking kill him.

James was just glad Tommy wasn't home. He would blow their cover for sure. The chicken shit was terrible at lying and had already been freaking out about the whole business. Two minutes with Tommy, and the detective would arrest the both of them.

There were three hard raps on the door. James supposed one wasn't enough to be heard and two was for friendly visits. Three was for business.

He opened the front door and sure as shit, there was a man holding out a detective's badge. He was a big one. Ain't no way James could take down a man like that. He wasn't ugly, even with his pathetic porn 'stache holding crumbs from what James guessed were donuts, but he wasn't a pretty boy neither. He looked arrogant, like he had all the answers to a test you didn't know you were about to take.

"Hello, I'm Detective Barnes with the Galveston County Sheriff's Office and I'm looking for a James Porter. Are you him?"

"Well that depends. Is he in trouble?"

"No, of course not. We're just tracking down some information. Did you ever or do you currently own a..." He pulled a small notebook out of his front pocket and flipped it open, checking his notes. "... 1984 white Chevy van?"

"Yeah, that's what I drive. What happened? Did someone steal my shit?" James poked his head out of the front door to try to see around the detective and into the street in front of his house. There was his van all right, parked halfway up on the curb. So why the hell did the dumb ass come up there with his questions if he could see the damn thing sitting right there?

Shit.

Maybe someone saw him that night down by the bridge. James' mind reeled. He needed to come up with something before the detective asked what he knew was probably coming next... where was he that night? He pulled his head back into the doorway but not before seeing Tommy round the corner at the bottom of the stairs. Fuck. He must have just gotten off work. Figures the one damn day he got off early to be the one time James didn't want him around.

"Sir, so that *is* your van sitting out front?" The detective moved aside and nodded a greeting as Tommy went into the house.

"Hey, Tommy! Uh yeah, that's my van." He put his arm around Tommy, gripping him tighter than he needed to, hoping he would get the hint. "This here's Tommy, Tommy, meet Detective Burns."

"Barnes, Detective Barnes."

"Yeah that's what I said. Tommy, Detective Burns was asking about my van down there but he didn't say why yet..." James looked at Barnes with wide eyes, "Detective, what's going on?"

The detective's eyes narrowed as he watched Tommy's face twitch in obvious distress. "We're just tracking down all older model van owners in the area. One was involved in an incident a few weeks ago."

"Oh shit, did I not pay the parking meter over on South Avenue? I was just popping in to Mikel's Pub for a quick beer, I was only parked there like five minutes."

"No sir, this was a bit more serious than that."

"What day was this 'incident', 'cause I was probably working or with Tommy here, we do everything together, ain't that right, Tommy?"

"Sure, I mean yeah... yeah we do everything together." Tommy gulped and avoided eye contact with the detective.

Barnes swatted a mosquito off his neck and looked down at his notebook. "Let's see now... June 8th, afternoon. It was a Friday." He looked back up at James and Tommy, "Where were you, Mr. Porter?"

"Hmm..." James rubbed his chin and looked past the detective. "Let's see, June 8th... wasn't that the day you and I went fishing, Tommy? Yeah, we was down on North Jetty, but the Rays kept taking all our bait. You remember, Tommy, you got that hook caught in your ear remember? See detective, there's still a scar right there on his ear."

The detective looked at Tommy who promptly held his shaggy blond hair back so he could see his ear. It wasn't a hook, but a damn cat that had ripped into the top of Tommy's ear. Mrs Donaldson's old black tomcat down at 240B, that fucking thing was always in their yard. Tommy was trying to pet it, the dumb ass, when he got the bright idea to pick it up and cuddle it. James was checking the mail when he heard the scream and looked up to see Tommy drop the cat and run to the house, blood trickling between the fingers clutching his ear. James waited until Mrs Donaldson was at her bingo game and shot the cat the next day. He threw the limp body into her trash can and covered it up with a pizza box. A few days later Mrs. Donaldson knocked on their door asking if they had seen the cat. James had laughed at her and said "Hell no, I hate cats," before slamming the door in her face. Tommy knew it wasn't a hook, but James caught his eye when the detective shuffled through that little notebook of his. Tommy knew when to shut up and listen and he was listening real good right then.

"Yep, sorry detective," Tommy touched the scar on his ear and straightened up as tall as he could. "We was fishin' all day together."

James clapped the detective on the shoulder, "See there, Detective Burns, it couldn't of been us. What happened anyway? Tommy and I love a juicy story. Was it in the papers? Tommy, I bet it was someone ran over that Mrs Donaldson's cat that she's been looking for."

The detective moved out from under James' hand, closed his notebook, and slowly put it back in his breast pocket. "Thanks for your cooperation, you boys have a good day." He turned and started back down the stairs before stopping. He swiveled around to face James and Tommy, still standing in the doorway. He cocked his head to the side, holding eye contact with James.

James winked and closed the door. He turned to face Tommy and whispered, "Now listen here, that's the story and you're fucking sticking to it okay? I don't want to hear any of your whiny bullshit."

"But James!" Tommy's face was turning red and his

eyes darted around, looking for his inhaler. "James, he knows! Oh my god, we're gonna go to jail! My mom's gonna kill me! What are we gonna do?"

James grabbed the inhaler from the kitchen counter and tossed it to Tommy. "Damnit, breathe before you pass out. We're not gonna do shit, I told you. Stick to the damn story. He don't know shit. He's gonna go back to eating his donuts and banging the girls that give him free coffee over by the putt putt, and you're gonna do nothing. Do you hear me, Tommy? Besides, we used fake names. Even if someone was there and heard something... they'll be looking for other people that ain't us."

"But James, he knows! Did you see his face? He knows we was lyin'! Shit, why'd I let you get me involved in this?" Tommy took a deep breath and pressed the inhaler down into its case, pumping the mist of medicine into his lungs.

"Because if I go down, you're going down with me. We were both there that night, or did you forget?"

"I wasn't the one that shot him!"

James took a step closer to Tommy, his voice low and level. "You're in this with me, Tommy. Now quit being a little bitch and just let it go. That fucker can't prove nothing, or we'd have left with him in the back of his fucking car. I'm telling you, we're golden."

10

————

Detective Barnes kept telling Rebecca they were doing everything they could, but she knew it wasn't enough. They still hadn't found Jon or found out anything else about what had happened that night. It was a busy road, but no one saw anything, or hadn't come forward if they did. All they knew was an old van had stopped, a car was washed clean of any evidence by the water, and a child was dead. Barnes was patient with her every time she called, when he did answer the phone. Lately it went straight to his voicemail. Of course he had to focus on the cases he could solve, and the people that he could catch. But it was her entire life. She had nothing to move on to.

She knew it was hopeless. In their eyes, anyway. Not worth the time spent tracking down dead ends. But Rebecca had all the time in the world. When she tried to go back to work, a few weeks earlier than planned, Paula had refused to allow it. It was a bitch move, Paula knew how much comfort Rebecca took from her work. But apparently everyone else knew what was best for her.

"You need more time, Becky," Paula had explained. "I'll call you in a few days to check on you. We're all praying for you."

Rebecca mumbled her goodbyes and slammed the phone down. She liked to work. She *needed* to work. She needed to think about something besides the thing that consumed her every minute of every day. At work, she knew what to do, what to focus on. At home it was another story. It wasn't fair. They knew how much she thrived on getting her work done, she had moved up in the company faster than anyone. That was Paula's problem, she realized. Paula was worried about her own job. Rebecca could take it, of course, if she wanted to. If they'd let her come back. If she was gone much longer, her projects would be finished by that shit-head David and he'd take all the credit for her hard work. But Paula wasn't budging.

So she took the time. In that empty house, with echoes of Oliver and Jon screaming at her, all she had was time. She wasn't sure what she should do with it, but she took it nonetheless. She spent most of her days sleeping late, then trudging to the coffee pot around noon. She would stand at the sink in the kitchen and look out the small window above it, staring at the backyard with its overgrown weeds and dirty jungle gym. After a few cups of coffee, she would land on the couch and binge episodes of old TV shows, not really listening to any of them.

Her clothes began to hang loosely on her small frame. What a diet plan, depression and grief. They should market that to the masses, she thought, as she wandered around the empty house. In the late evening moments between dinner and failed attempts at sleep, she wondered if she would ever find her 'normal' again.

It wasn't a large home by anyone's standards, but it felt enormous to Rebecca. Everywhere she turned, memories of a stolen life assaulted her. Some days it took her thirty minutes to walk down the hallway past Oliver's room. She would pause there at his door, a smile threatening to grab the corner of her mouth as she thought of the day she helped him make the sign still taped there. He wanted to do the writing himself, and he was only four, so it was a slow process. But when he finished, there was his name in three-inch-tall bold blue crayon letters. But that small sliver of hope that it was all a bad dream faded as soon as she opened the door to an empty room. Dust would stir up with the gentle push of air from the hallway, floating around in the beam of sunlight coming in through his large window, before settling onto the toys that lay scattered on his floor. They lay there, waiting for him to come back and finish playing with them. The bed, soft blankets in the race car frame, screamed at her to bring him back. His pillow case, halfway off the pillow, still carried the scent of bubble gum shampoo. Pale blue walls adorned with cartoon posters glared at her. His closet, the door halfway open revealing dirty clothes in a heap on the floor, blamed her. She tried to stay out of his room, but she was torn between wanting to remember every moment, and not wanting to drown in the pain of missing him. Most days she went in, lay on his bed with her head on his pillow, and closed her eyes. With the scent of his shampoo wafting around her, she pretended he was just down the hall, taking a bath. Any minute he would come barreling down the hallway and jump onto the bed with her, wanting a bedtime story. Jon was usually the one who did that, but she would give anything to go back in time and just read him one. But every day the bubble gum faded a little more, and she knew she was losing him.

And Jon... she knew Jon was gone. She knew the same way she knew he was the one she wanted to spend the rest of her life with, after that second date. But those were happier times, before mortgages and jobs got in the way. Back when they could talk for hours and couldn't wait to see each other every day after work. They had lost a lot of who they were, in trying to have Ollie. Years of taking her temperature and peeing on strips to see when she was ovulating. Endless doctor appointments explaining why, even if Jon's sperm count was high enough, her uterus was an inhospitable environment and their chances were slim. They pinned their happiness and their future on that small sliver of hope. Sex became a means to an end, and there was a palpable tension as each one blamed the other for their inability to have children. They had just started adoption paperwork when she discovered she was pregnant with Oliver. He was all they focused on or talked to each other about. He was the only thing holding them together. It was a big burden to carry for a child, but he held it up. She wondered what would happen if... when... they found Jon. With their glue gone, left at the bottom of that canal, would they fall apart? She wasn't sure.

Days passed with more headlines and more pressing issues. Rebecca understood, as her phone calls to Detective Barnes trickled to a stop. A sixteen-year-old girl over in Texas City had disappeared into the night, but they were leaning towards her being a runaway. It was the parents' fault, Rebecca knew. They should have watched her closer, should have seen the signs. In Pearland, an eighth grader brought a hand gun to school. He didn't shoot anyone, just wanted to show his friends, look cool. The parents should have locked it up tighter where he couldn't get to it. Then, just a few neighborhoods over from her, a pregnant woman was crossing the street and a Ford Escort came out of nowhere, plowed right over her, and kept going. She didn't make it. Rebecca knew there were more urgent matters, ones that might have better outcomes that the media and police needed to focus on. It was how the world worked. Police prioritized their cases, and every day Jon and Oliver slipped lower on that list. But she needed to find Jon, in whatever condition. It was the not knowing that hurt the most. Not knowing if he was alive, or out there hurting. She knew the detective thought Jon was gone, a lost cause. They'd found blood on the ground. They were waiting for forensics to be sure it was Jon's. It wasn't a lot, anyway, not enough for him to have bled to death, but he had been attacked. And that was enough for them to slow the search, to assume the worst. She lived her life in limbo, unable to move on. And she needed to know what happened to Oliver, because that was the part that was so impossible to imagine. Why would anyone kill a child? What led to that moment, when they decided her sweet little boy didn't deserve to live?

So she wandered the empty home, and wondered why her baby was killed, and knew Jon wasn't coming back. She didn't know how to *be* anymore. Some days she had to remind herself to breathe, to eat, to try to sleep. But she couldn't bear to sleep in their bed alone, staring at an empty spot where Jon should have been. His shampoo faded from the pillow with each passing day. She took his pillow to the couch and lay on it face down, inhaling the cotton fibers in a desperate attempt to hold onto him. Wrapped in Oliver's comforter, head resting on Jon's pillow, tears would course down her face. Every few days, when her body couldn't physically function anymore... she would finally fall into a fitful sleep. But even then, she couldn't escape the pain. As soon as her eyes closed, a new nightmare would begin. Her husband in pain, her son crying out to her for help... until she would wake up, sobbing. She lost all track of time, and only knew the afternoons by the sight of the mailman's shadow and the rustle of mail dropping into the box by their front door. Time didn't matter, anyway. She no longer needed to know when Oliver would want his lunch, or when Jon would be home from work. No one needed her.

She went through the photo albums, skimming past the holes left from the missing pictures. Detective Barnes should return them soon, she needed to put them back. The empty sleeves screamed at her every time she turned the pages, showing a broken family. She stopped at a picture she had taken the previous summer, on a rare day when all three of them were at the beach together. Jon was lying down as Oliver poured buckets of sand on top of his body. They were both looking at the camera, their matching blue eyes twinkling as they laughed. She slid the photograph from the protective slip and touched Oliver's face, catching a tear before it fell onto the picture. Her whole body ached with longing as she struggled to take a breath. She tucked the picture into her purse and grabbed her keys. She needed to see the place where her Ollie was last happy and alive.

11

Rebecca was almost to the bridge, almost to the spot where Oliver had died. She held her breath and stared straight ahead, pushing harder on the gas pedal. Her black Ford Escort rumbled past the side road that ended at the canal, the water that took her Ollie. She zipped up the bridge, going faster than she ever had, hoping no one was on the other side of it, going slower than they needed to. Her car cleared the top, and still she stared ahead, missing the fantastic view that she usually loved. No one was on the other side.

The guard leaned out of the small window of their shack to get a look at Rebecca's beach permit stuck to the front windshield of her car. He nodded and she drove through, over the thickly packed sand, and took a left onto the beach towards their spot. On one side were the dunes, where the tips of discarded Christmas trees still poked up above the sand. The trees were the city's attempt to build the dunes back up, after years of high tides had reduced them to small mounds. Dunes were critical to keeping the storm surges back from the beach houses and small businesses there on the waterfront. Some people chose to park there, close to the mound of trees and sand, but the Crows never did. It was too dangerous to let Ollie cross the road to the beach on her right. They usually backed up a few feet from the tide, with enough room between their car's open trunk and the water to place their chairs, umbrella, and Oliver's toys.

After scanning the water, Rebecca finally found what she was looking for. A partially submerged boat, about twenty feet out. There were a handful of local legends about how it got there, and what had happened to the crew. Part of their trips always included listening to Oliver come up with a new story. His eyes would light up as he described pirates, giant squid, and sharks. They never did look up the real reason for it, and she had a feeling she never would. She was happy to stick with Oliver's imaginative versions.

She eased her car onto the loose sand near the sunken boat and stopped close to the water's edge. Stepping out of her car, a burst of hot salty air and suntan lotion immediately hit her. Breathing it in, she blinked back tears. Seagulls immediately swept down hoping for the stray bits of food they were used to getting from the beach visitors. Oliver loved to fling his food up into their open beaks where they would gobble up the potato chips and small pieces of bread torn from his sandy peanut butter and jelly sandwiches. He would throw them as high as his little arms could launch, laughing as the birds hurried to see who would get to it first. Squealing with delight, he would watch them dart up and down, calling to each other.

"Did you know a group of seagulls is called a colony?" Jon would say, always eager for a teachable moment.

"Yes, we know. You say that every time we're here," Rebecca would respond, rolling her eyes.

Oliver would laugh and yell, "Seagull Colonly! Come here Colonly!"

Every. Single. Time.

Then, without missing a beat, Jon would lean in and whisper to Rebecca, "It's better than being called a 'Murder', eh? Rebecca *Crow*?" and wink at her.

Every. Single. Time.

The birds flew around her as she stood there, zipping down before darting back up into the sky. If a seagull could be disappointed, she imagined it would look something like them at that moment. Rebecca wondered if any of them had been there that day, that awful day the last time Jon and Oliver were in that same spot. She leaned against her car and slipped out of her worn flip-flops, wriggling her feet and burying her toes into the soft sand. The sand was warm, but not quite hot. Not as hot as it would be later that afternoon, when you didn't dare walk on it barefoot. They had spent many trips carrying Oliver back and forth across the sand after watching him hop-scream-hop across the steaming ground.

Near her toes was a small hole. Rebecca crouched down to dig out a hermit crab, wrapped tightly in its shell. She held it there in her hand until it became brave again, and tiny brown feet tickled her palm as it explored the air outside of the shell.

"Hey little guy, don't worry, I'll put you back."

She eased the crab back onto the sand near the hole and stood up, brushing her hands off on her shorts. Oliver would have placed it in his jar and stared at it through the magnifying glass lid. He would have named it something silly like 'Pickles' and would have cried when she insisted he put it back when it was time for them to go home.

Her breath caught in her throat as she moved towards the tide. She shuffled in the shallow water parallel to the shore, trying to imagine what Jon and Oliver did there that Friday. The beach around her came to life as the sun moved higher in the sky and people poured out of vehicles, eager to enjoy their day. Kids sprinted towards the water as adults caught up with them, pulling them back to the cars and lathering their arms and legs with sunscreen. Chairs unfolded with a clank and bikini-clad bodies plopped down, pushing the plastic chair legs further into the sand. Some pulled out books to read in the shade of their umbrellas, while others helped their kids build sandcastles. Smaller children were carried into the water, their arms sticking straight out from their sides by the addition of inflatable swimming cuffs.

Everyone was smiling. Everyone was alive.

She turned her back on the crowds and eased into the shallow surf. The water tickled; first her calves, then her knees as she continued walking. Broken shells and sand shifted underneath her feet as something skittered against the edge of her heel. Gentle rolling waves lapped at the edges of her shorts before creeping up her thighs. Once she felt the shock of cooler water on her stomach through her thin shirt, she bent her knees and let herself drop into the water up to her neck. Echoes of happy families faded as she swam further out. She stopped once her feet could no longer touch the bottom. Rebecca rolled onto her back and stretched her arms out, facing the clouds above her. With the incoming waves to her right, and the beach to her left, she floated. Each swell caressed her as it passed underneath, before breaking as it moved closer to the shoreline. The sun had risen to its full height by then, and the rays beat down on her face as the water held her body up effortlessly. High above her, soft white clouds drifted by, and seagulls floated on the breeze.

The ocean had always been home for her. Its rhythms were her heartbeat. There was nowhere else she felt more at peace, but it wasn't working that day. She pulled her arms back to her sides and let her body sink into the water, then pushed up to propel herself downward. It was murky, and too sandy to see very far in front of her. She held her arms out and kept pushing up to keep her body beneath the surface. A vast emptiness surrounded her while the tide pulled and pushed her body. In one direction were the beach, her car, and her empty home. In the other, miles and miles of nothing but the ocean.

The realization that Oliver was gone didn't come in the heart-wrenching moment she saw his small arm draped on the back seat of Jon's car. It didn't even come at the funeral, when his pale little body lay surrounded by cold white silk. Rather, it came in the million little things that built up around her and swallowed her whole until she found herself in the middle of the ocean, surrounded by emptiness, and no idea how she had gotten there.

Her wedding ring slipped down her recently thinned finger as she continued to wave her arms to stay below the surface of the water. She pushed the ring back frantically and floated to the surface, her arms no longer able to keep her down. Her wet hair broke the surface first, then her face, with a loud gasp as her lungs filled with the much-needed air. Treading water with a crooked finger to make sure the ring didn't slip again, she considered sinking back down into the peaceful abyss. But the weight of her ring pulled her back. She needed to be there for Jon, for when he came home. If there was even the smallest chance that he was still alive, she couldn't leave him.

She turned towards the shore and started to swim.

Rebecca didn't notice, or didn't care, that sea water drenched her driver's seat, or that her clothes clung to her thin body. She drove back towards the bridge with one mission, to trace their last steps and try to find some answers. She wondered what they would have talked about in the car on that same road. Oliver would have sung along with the radio, the windows rolled down and the wind drying his sandy blond hair as they drove. Sitting in the middle seat, even with his booster, he couldn't see very far out of the windows, so Jon would announce when they were going over the big bridge. Oliver's eyes would light up. He loved bridges.

Turning left, she pulled off the highway and turned

her car around towards the water's edge. A yellow piece of police tape was flapping in the wind like a beacon, snagged on a bit of driftwood. The water was choppy and murky, and as she got out of her car and walked to its edge, she couldn't see very far down into the darkness. She tried to imagine Jon's car down there, filling up with water while a frightened Oliver cried out for her. She had failed him.

Turning from the water, Rebecca scanned the area. The setting sun reflected a golden hue on everything, and the bridge rumbled as cars drove by. She could almost make out the top of a bait shop in the distance, positioned next to the old boat ramps. Jon would have gotten out of his car to check for the spare in the trunk. Rebecca shook her head, still angry at herself for not replacing it. She went to the rear of the car and opened the trunk. There was the spare to her own car, tucked away beneath the mat.

The Ford dipped down as she sat on the edge of the open trunk and watched the cars speed by. "The man who killed Ollie is out there, right now," she thought. "He's alive and breathing and living his life while I sit here, picturing Jon and Oliver's last day together." It wasn't fair. Something had to happen soon or she would go insane. He was free. He wasn't missing his family, he wasn't waiting around for anything. He was free. He should have been suffering as much as she was.

He shouldn't get to be free.

As she watched the cars go by, her eyes locked on a white van. It was old, and Jon said it had looked rough. What if that was the van that stopped to help him? What if that was the man who killed them? It clearly wasn't AAA who stopped that night. That van was responsible, she just knew it. Jon's guard was down because he thought it was AAA and that van was carrying the man who killed them.

Jon was still missing, Oliver's killer was still out there,

and it was starting to look like he would get away with it.

She was tired of waiting for the police. She slammed the trunk and got back into her car. Pulling up onto the highway, she headed for home. For the first time in a long time, she knew exactly what she needed to do.

12

———

James had only been to see his mom's landlord, Martin, a couple of times. A few years back his mama had stepped in a hole in her backyard and broken her ankle, so he offered to deliver rent for her. A hole that happened to be dug by her new dog, Cooper. The dog was a damn nuisance. James told her it wasn't a good idea to get the mutt, all he did was bark at nothing and dig holes. With tan wiry hair, and a tail permanently tucked between his legs, the thing even looked useless. But his mama thought having a dog made her safer, in case anyone wanted to break in and steal... what? Her social security check? Everyone in the Third Ward knew she didn't have anything worth taking. James told her she didn't need another mouth to feed, and she really didn't need all that barking. That fucking dog yelped at everything, night and day. It's a wonder the neighbors didn't poison it.

He took care of that before they ever had a chance to.

When he got back home from taking his mama to the emergency room the night she broke her ankle (and spent most of that week's paycheck), he helped her into bed, careful not to jostle the boot on her left leg and waited for her to fall asleep. She was doped up on painkillers, so sleep came quickly. Then he went to her garage and found a spool of rope. It was pretty old, and there was no telling what she had originally bought it for. She always had ideas for shit around the house, most of which James ended up doing. But he figured it would do. He cut a few pieces off the spool and headed to the backyard. There was the damn dog, staring at the fence and barking into the night air at absolutely nothing.

"Come here Coop! Come here, boy!"

The dog stopped barking and turned to look at James, ears pointed straight up and his body stiff. The damn thing had never liked him, and hell if he knew why. Well, he wasn't gonna wait around all night for him to get over that. James stood up and walked to the stake in the ground holding the dog's chain. He picked up the chain and followed the end of it all the way to the dog, stopping when he had his hand on Cooper's dirty blue collar. James wrapped one piece of rope around the dog's muzzle first, so he'd stop the goddamn barking. He didn't need his mama waking up, she needed her rest. It wriggled and whined the whole time, but he was finally able to tie the front legs together next. James sat on the side of the dog's chest while he tied up the rear legs. He stepped back to observe his work, feeling pretty good about the knots. Fuck the boy scouts, he didn't need to sit around a circle jerk to know how to tie a knot.

Leaving the dog lying in the grass, whimpering and wide eyed, James headed back to the garage. The shovel was there, leaning against the wall behind the door. James grabbed it. If the dog wanted to dig holes, he would be more than happy to help him out. He found a soft spot of ground and dug down a few feet. The dog was heavier than he thought and by the time he got it over to the loose dirt, he was out of breath. He dropped the dog into the hole where it landed with a thud and a muffled yelp. He had to admit, the thing had spunk. It kept fighting those knots and moving around, whining through closed jaws with wide eyes.

James checked his watch, it was almost time to meet up with Tommy over at Mikel's and he didn't want to be late. He took one last look at the dog as he jumped to his feet and dusted the dirt off the knees of his jeans. It was kind of cute, he could see why his mama got the thing, but it was just too much damn trouble.

Cooper's moves became more frantic as James

shoveled dirt back into the hole on top of him. With each shovel full, the dog moved less and less, until he was completely still. It didn't take as long to fill the hole as it had taken to dig it, especially with the damn dog taking up most of the room. He put the shovel back in the garage and wiped his hands on his jeans. No more barking, no more holes for his mama to trip in.

The next morning, James told his mama he accidentally left the gate open, but she knew her son well enough to know there was more to the story. She let it go, as she was used to doing, and ignored the freshly dug hole in her backyard. He had to deliver her rent checks for a few months until her ankle healed up, but she never got another dog, and he hadn't seen Martin much since then.

***

James knocked on the green door of Martin's house. A chain rattled off its lock before the door opened a few inches and small brown eyes stared at him through the gap. Recognition flashed, and the door opened wider.

"Hey, aren't you Sandra Porter's boy? You here to deliver more rent checks? What, did she go and break her ankle again?"

"Yeah I'm her boy and no, I'm not delivering the rent." James crossed the threshold.

Martin took a step back, away from James. "Well I told her I wasn't gonna wait around all month. You tell her I'm serious about her paying."

James looked around the living room, "Where's your bitch? Out spending your money?"

"Now wait a damn minute, you can't just come in here like that! Get the hell out of my house before I call the cops."

"It's all right, I already saw her down at Boudreaux's on my way here. I know you're all alone." James grinned.

Martin stepped back with his hands raised in front of him, towards the kitchen and away from James. "Look, I don't want any trouble. You want an extension for your mama? No problem. Tell her she can have another week."

James chuckled "I don't believe you. As soon as I leave here you're going to have her evicted and you know it." He slowly moved his hand around to the back of his waistband and rested his fingertips on the cold handle of his dad's old Beretta M9.

"Look, just leave, okay? She can take all the time she needs." Martin glanced around nervously.

James pulled the gun out from behind his back and held it loosely at his side.

Martin's eyes widened as he saw the gun. "Oh whoa, what are you doing? Seriously, man? Come on, we can talk about it."

"Oh, but I don't think we can. I think we're done here. I think you're done giving my mom a hard time."

James got a shot off before Martin ever saw him raise the gun.

Blood poured from between his fingers as he clutched his stomach. He looked up at James in disbelief. "You fucking SHOT me!? What the hell?" He stumbled into the kitchen, bloody hands grasping at drawer handles, leaving red swipes on everything he touched.

James shot two more rounds off into Martin's back, one after the other like he was pinning a tail on a donkey. The stench of copper and gun powder filled the space between them.

Blood gurgled up, blocking whatever words Martin was trying to form as he slumped onto the cold tiles of the kitchen floor. His mouth opened and closed like a guppy, hands still feeling around for some sort of weapon. James knelt beside him and touched the barrel of the gun to Martin's chin, forcing him to look up. He met Martin's eyes as he said, "I never did like you." He pulled the trigger one last time. Smoke curled from Martin's open mouth, his nose, and the jagged hole in his neck as pieces of his scalp and thinning hair spread out onto the cabinets behind him.

James carefully wiped down everything he had touched and let himself out, marveling at how easily it had all come back to him. He hadn't fired his gun since he killed that man down by the canal, and before that hadn't fired it since that night with his dad. It's funny how easy things get, once you get some practice in.

He drove home, wondering if Martin's bitch liked cleaning up as much as she liked shopping.

13

———

Rebecca sat cross-legged on the floor in the middle of the walk-in closet she used to share with Jon. Rows of clothing surrounded her, his on the right and hers on the left. Shoe boxes half full of receipts, old pictures, and random papers lay scattered around her like confetti. It had to be there somewhere. She knew Jon like the back of her hand. Even after insisting he get rid of the thing, she knew the sentimental value would weigh on him heavier than her anger.

When his dad died, and his mother still had all of her faculties about her, Claire had given Jon his dad's pistol. The same pistol that they would take to the gun range when he was younger. He talked about how much he loved those days with his dad, where he didn't answer work calls, or watch football games over Jon's little head. It was the only quality time they had together. When he died, and his mother asked if he wanted it, he wouldn't have hesitated before saying 'of course', regardless of how Rebecca felt about guns in their home. It was months before he even mentioned it, letting it slip one night during one of their heated arguments about something stupid. Oliver was a baby, only six months old, and nowhere near the age of walking around and getting into things, but Rebecca adamantly refused to have a gun in their home. Rebecca knew Jon had grown up around guns and knew how to handle them safely. They did live in Texas, after all, where everyone had a gun in their nightstand and boots in their closet. But she hadn't grown up comfortable with them, and the thought of Oliver coming into contact with one of the things terrified her. There was that one kid in a Houston suburb who shot and killed his brother with his dad's gun. They were playing around, neither one understanding the danger. The bullet had hit the younger brother in the neck, killing him instantly. Just like that, he was gone. A mother left without a son, a boy without his brother. Not that Oliver would ever have a brother, or a brother would ever have Oliver... not anymore.

She was down to the last shoe box on the top shelf, the one marked '2015 receipts'. When she picked it up, it was much heavier than a box of papers had any right to be. She carried it with her back to the floor, removed the lid, and started pulling out papers. There it was, at the bottom next to a box of ammunition.

Rebecca sat in the middle of the closet holding the gun in her hands. The cold weight of it surprised her; she had never held one before. She had never needed to hold one before her world shattered and left her with nothing but a quiet house, an unused side of the bed, and dust-covered toys. Before the man who took everything from her was allowed to walk around like nothing had happened. Before the police decided to do nothing about it.

It took her a few days of watching videos online before she could load and unload the weapon. She learned how to check if a round was in the chamber, and how to cock it. But she didn't learn how to be comfortable with it, the heavy thing in her hands. It was still so foreign to her, and she wasn't sure she'd even know what to do with it when the time came. But it was something. She had to do something. She couldn't just keep sitting there waiting for police to find an invisible man. She would have to find her own justice. She knew he drove a van, and with no one at home, and a boss who still wouldn't let her return to work, she had nothing but time. She had to find that van.

***

She set out in her car the next day to look for answers.

Morrison crooned from her radio as she drove down the highway. With the windows down, the wind rushed across her face and each breath brought the taste of salty sea air. A flicker of movement from the backseat caught her eye. It was Oliver, grinning at her and reaching his little hand as far out the window as he could reach. His small fingers waved in the bit of air he was able to catch. Tears sprang into her eyes as she stared at his reflection. The car came to a stop in the middle of the highway.

Rebecca turned around to face the seat behind her, but Oliver was gone. An eighteen wheeler careened around her, laying on its horn. Startled, she turned back to the road, took a deep breath, and pressed on the gas again.

"I'll get him, Ollie," she promised. "I'll get him, and everything will be fine again."

She scanned the feeders and side roads. The sun beat down on everything with harsh, unrelenting rays. Heat shimmered off the road in iridescent waves, and even the birds had taken a sabbatical from flying. She could see them resting in the shade along the roadside.

Her console suddenly flashed, an incoming call from Detective Barnes. She pressed a button on the screen to accept his call.

"Hello detective, any news?" Rebecca started off every call from him with the same greeting.

His sigh echoed around her as it came through the car's speakers. "I'm sorry Mrs Crow, we're doing everything we can. Just wanted to touch base and let you know I'm still working on finding your husband. We're running down every van in the area, but so far they all check out."

"I understand," she replied, irritated. "Please call me if you find anything"

"Of course I will."

She jammed her finger against the button, ending the call. She missed the days of being able to slam down a receiver in anger. It seemed to Rebecca that she was right when she stopped putting her faith in the police, since there didn't appear to be any progress in the weeks since Oliver was killed, and Jon had gone missing. Plus it gave her a reason to get off the couch every day and out of that house. Otherwise, she would lay there thinking of Oliver and Jon and feeling sorry for herself, and that wouldn't help anyone. It sure wasn't helping her find Jon. But this... this she could do. Maybe.

She pulled to the side of the road, on the other side of the bridge from where Jon's car went into the water. She hoped the killer took this road to work, or it was a regular route for him. She was counting on it, anyway. She turned the car just enough underneath the bridge to have shade but not so much that she wasn't visible from the road. Rebecca shifted into park and turned the car off with a click. She left the windows down so it wouldn't get too hot inside, and popped the trunk. She moved jackets and blankets to the side and found the latch for the compartment holding her spare. It seemed easy enough, she thought, feeling a pang of guilt at the sight of the spare tire. If she had only replaced Jon's, he and Ollie might still be alive. Shaking off the thought, she tried to focus. She removed the tire wrench from its slot and left the trunk open. She hoped that would make her car a little easier to see from the highway. She leaned against the rear of the car as she held the tire iron, swatted mosquitoes, and watched cars as they sped by.

It was late afternoon, around the same time of day Jon and Oliver had pulled off the highway. It was Tuesday instead of Friday, but she hoped that didn't matter. Rebecca watched as the cars and trucks rolled by, heading to their families or homes or activities. There were a lot of trucks, but it was Texas so that wasn't unusual. She listened to the tires on the pavement, and the faint groans from the bridge as they passed over her. Thirty minutes passed before she saw a car exit the freeway and head in her direction. Frustrated, she waited for it to pull up. It was a small yellow Kia, not a van. A well-dressed young man stepped out, tall and trim.

"Hey there, need some help?"

Rebecca waved her hand and put on her best smile, "No thanks, I've got it."

"You sure? I don't mind" He pulled at his suit jacket, whipping it off with a practiced flourish.

"No, really, I'm okay. I don't need you." Her smile faltered.

He paused at the directness in her voice, still holding his jacket. "Okay, well... good luck then."

He pulled his jacket back on and returned to his car, reversing until he was back on the highway. She wondered how long she would have to stand there before the man in the van showed up, if he did at all. She knew she was grasping at straws, but it was the only thing she could think of to do.

A silver Cougar, a white Escort, a black F150, and a Blue Ram all showed up, in that order. Each time they offered to help her, and each time she insisted she was okay. All four had driven off confused. Her plan wasn't working. She knew the chances were slim that the man in the van would risk stopping there again. Her stomach growled and she touched it in surprise. It was the first day since the accident, that she actually felt hungry. Standing in the heat all afternoon and most of the evening had left her parched and famished. And with nothing to show for it. She tossed the tire wrench back in the trunk with a clang and slammed the lid closed before heading around to the driver's side door.

"Need help?"

Rebecca turned towards the voice, startled. She hadn't heard tires on the gravel, or the van's motor at all. And it was definitely a van. Right in front of her, a clunky avocado-green van. Well, mostly green. A few panels were still primer gray. The man in front of her was tall, with wavy black hair, and a devious smile. Dressed in jeans, work boots, and a long-sleeved button-up, Rebecca realized he could be anyone. He could be a pipe fitter at one of the plants out there, or a mechanic, or... a killer.

Rebecca took a deep breath and hoped the man didn't see her heart threatening to break through her chest. She forced a smile and replied, "Yes, that would be great!"

"I'm Leon." He reached out a hand to shake hers. "What seems to be the trouble?"

"Ah... just a flat. I have a spare in the trunk." She shook his hand and her stomach rose in her throat at his touch. She jerked her arm back to her side.

"Oh good, that's an easy fix." He winked at her as he knelt to look at the closest tire. "Which tire is it?"

Of course he would wink, he was going to take advantage of her, or rob her, or whatever his sick mind had decided to do. Disgusted, she turned away from him and scrambled for an answer. She hadn't thought this far into her obviously flawed plan. Her tires were all clearly full of air. She scratched at a mosquito bite on her arm to buy some time.

"Damn mosquitos, you don't happen to have any spray, do you? I left mine at home."

"Sure! I don't leave home without it. Hold on, I'll go grab it."

She realized, too late, that she had given him the perfect excuse to go to his van and grab a weapon. Or to get one out of his pocket, or wherever he kept it.

It was the man, she was sure of it. He was smooth enough to disguise his motives. Jon would have trusted him since he was being so helpful. Until he revealed himself to be the monster he really was.

It was the man who had attacked her Ollie and Jon.

14

"Hey, are you still in town? Looks like the AAA guy is here already, we'll just ride with him. You can meet us at the mechanic shop, it's closer to home anyway."

"I'm not, but I can turn around. They got there fast."

"Yeah, I thought so too. But he's not in a tow truck. This is probably the car service so we don't have to ride with the tow guy. Either way, they really need to invest in nicer vehicles. This van looks like it's about to fall apart. I'll call you back when we're on the road again. Love you."

As the old green van pulled in closer, Jon turned to his open trunk and scowled at a gaping round hole where the spare tire should have been. He slammed the trunk lid shut as the man stepped out of the van. Wearing dusty work boots, worn jeans, and a long-sleeved shirt, he certainly looked the part of an auto repairman. Or was it tow man? Jon didn't know how they categorized themselves. He was tall, with almost curly black hair and a friendly smile.

The man reeked of mosquito spray as he held his hand out to shake Jon's. "I'm Leon, looks like you're having a bit of trouble, need some help?"

Jon looked at him, confused, as he lifted his arm to shake his outstretched hand. The weight of his hand surprised him and he looked down to see he was still holding the tire iron. He shifted it to his other hand, and shook. Of course he needed help, that's why he called them. "Um, yeah. You sure got here fast; I just hung up about fifteen minutes ago."

Leon's thick eyebrows drew together. "What's that?"

As Jon began explaining his call to AAA, the man interrupted him. "Oh, that makes sense now. No, I'm not with them. I was just driving by and saw you stopped here. Looked like you could use a hand."

"Thanks, but they really should be here any minute."

"It's okay," Leon insisted, smiling. He took the tire iron from Jon's grasp. "I don't mind."

Jon studied the other man's face. "No, it's really okay, but thank you."

Jon reached for the tire iron, but Leon swung it out of reach and his grin widened. "What's wrong, man? I'm helping you here!"

Jon took a step sideways, putting himself between Oliver and the man, and held his palms out. "Look, I don't want any trouble."

Jon glanced towards the car, thankful that Oliver was finally being quiet. It was humid and scorching outside, so the air conditioner in the Chevy was on full blast. Oliver had protested when Jon rolled the windows up, but he wanted to keep the cold air in as much as possible. Praying he stayed that quiet, Jon took a deep breath and reminded himself to stay calm. He was about eighty percent sure the guy was not a good Samaritan, stopping to aid a troubled traveler. But that twenty percent. That twenty percent is what worried him. What if he was overreacting? What if he just let him help and then he would be on his way? He watched Jon, as Jon watched him, both men hoping to figure out the puzzle but having very different ideas of what a good outcome would be.

Oliver picked that moment to call out from the backseat of the car, breaking the tension. "Daaaaadd!"

Leon glanced towards the car, looked back at Jon, and laughed as he handed the tire iron back to him. "Hey relax, I'm just messin' with ya!"

Jon forced a chuckle and held the tool at his side, hoping the man would leave soon.

Leon moved towards his van as if to go, turning to face Jon when he opened the driver's side door. "Hope you get on the road okay, good luck to you." He leaned into the van as if to pull himself up into the driver's seat. Jon exhaled the breath he hadn't realized he was holding and turned towards the car to answer Oliver. "I'm here buddy, shouldn't be much longer and we'll be ho…"

A white heat exploded in Jon's back before his ears could register the shot.

He dropped to the ground. Gravel dug into his knees and he gasped as blood gurgled from his mouth onto hands that seemed to be someone else's. Blood rolled between his fingers to the dust below. Jon pulled his hands in, trying to get a grasp of what was happening. Oliver cried out for him, his voice shaking with fear. Jon tried to respond, but all that he could get out was a wet cough, sputtering blood onto the front of his shirt and the dirt below him.

Jon tried to turn to face the man as he heard footsteps behind him, but a hard boot on his back pushed him flat into the dirt. Dust crept into Jon's mouth and nose as he struggled to rise. Leaning down close to Jon's ear, Leon whispered, "Let's not make a scene, shall we? Wouldn't want to scare the kid." A rock cut into his ear as he lay there, head turned towards the flat tire, no longer able to move. He tried again to call out to Oliver, but the blood had mingled with the dirt, creating a thick heavy paste inside his mouth.

There was a tug on his jeans as Leon pulled a wallet from Jon's back pocket with a jerk. "Oliver..." Jon managed to mumble, but no one heard him. The man was already in his van. His tires threw dirt into the air as he spun around to get back onto the road before anyone came poking around. The van soon joined the low hum of traffic crossing over the bridge.

Jon hoped the AAA guys would be there soon to take Oliver back to Rebecca safe and sound. He knew it was too late for him. Every breath was harder to draw in, and the warmth coming from his chest seemed to radiate out to the rest of his body, enveloping him. As Jon exhaled one more painful breath, he thought he heard a quiet click coming from the backseat of the car.

Oliver knew he would be in trouble for unbuckling the seat belt that stretched across his booster seat, but he needed to find his dad. Something was wrong, his dad always answered him when he cried out. He climbed out of the seat and pulled himself up to the edge of the window. Nothing. He tried the door handle, but it never opened for him in the back, so he crawled over the console to the front seats, dragging his stuffed elephant along with him. He sat on his knees and set his hands on the steering wheel, trying to see over it. There was water in front of him, and the bridge above that and to the left. He thought he could feel the car shake as a large truck rumbled overhead. Oliver's chin started to quiver, and he looked around again for his dad. No one ever left him alone like that. He wasn't sure what he should do. He sat in the driver's seat, his eyes wide and glistening with tears that threatened to spill over. He needed to get home to his mommy; she would help him find his dad.

Cold air blew on his face from the vent as he leaned over to touch the gear shifter. He remembered his dad moving this around before but wasn't sure which way it was supposed to go, or how it worked. He wiggled it but it didn't budge from its spot next to the big 'P'. Oliver knew his letters, his teacher at preschool made him and his friends go over them every day. That was definitely a 'P'. P stood for... Puppies... and... Pumpkins! He smiled as he remembered the pictures on the wall at school. There were some other letters there with the P, and he traced them all with his finger. He hadn't learned all of them yet. He jiggled the stick, but again it refused to move. Frustrated, he sat back in the seat and stared at it. There was a button on the side, he realized, and reached out to push it. Again, nothing happened. Maybe he wasn't pushing it hard enough. He leaned forward and gripped the stick with both hands, pulling down as hard as he could. With a jolt, the stick moved down to the "D" spot. Oliver smiled as the car inched forward. He did it! He was moving! But as the water inched closer, the smile dropped from his face and his eyes widened. He needed to go in the other direction. He was moving towards the water, not the road.

"Daaaaaaaaaaaad!!!" He looked out the window again, but still couldn't see his dad. Oliver grabbed the stick again, pushing and pulling to try to get it to move to a different letter, not knowing what he had done the first time to get it to move.

Jon's eyes fluttered behind closed lids as he heard Oliver's scream. With a burst of adrenaline, he pulled his hands toward his body and pushed up from the ground. He couldn't stand, but he could pull his legs up enough to crawl towards the car. He inched forward.

The car dipped down as the front wheels left the embankment, pushing Oliver forward into the steering wheel. The water rushed closer, covering the front of the car. He pounded on the window, screaming for his dad to help. He could finally see him, there on the ground, but he wasn't getting up, he wasn't helping. He caught his dad's eye and waved at him through the window. He saw him! Oliver knew his dad would come fix this... but he wasn't getting up. His dad was crawling towards the water like a baby and looking at Oliver, crying. His face was all dirty and twisted up. He lost sight of his dad as the car jolted one more time, left the bank completely, and sank into the brackish water.

Once the car stopped tipping forward and had settled in the water, Oliver crawled back to the back seat, dragging Sammy along with him. He settled into his booster seat with the stuffed elephant on his lap. The car gently rocked as the water crept up, tickling Oliver's bare feet. He pulled his knees up to his chest, crushing Sammy who was sitting on his lap, wrapped his arms around his legs, and lowered his face into Sammy's blue fur.

15

———

Rebecca blinked rapidly to see through the tears that had filled her eyes. Shuddering, she took a deep breath and looked at the back of the man who killed her family.

"Why?" she screamed at him, "Why did you have to kill them?"

The man stopped, his hand on the van door, and spun around, "What?"

"He was just a baby! And you could have just taken Jon's wallet; he would have given it to you! You didn't have to kill him!"

Leon held his arms out in front of him, and stared at Rebecca's hand, "Lady, I have no idea what you're talking about, but we can figure this out. Just put the gun down."

Rebecca looked down at her white knuckles clutched around the handle of her late father-in-law's gun. She couldn't remember grabbing it from the car, cocking it, or raising it towards Leon.

Leon opened the door to his van with a soft click. She looked up into his eyes, wide with fright. She tilted her head to the side, maybe it wasn't the guy... maybe it was... but she couldn't chance it. Everything went quiet as she took a deep breath. Rebecca gripped her hand around the gun, closed her eyes, and squeezed the trigger. The gun kicked backwards as she fired, and the noise bounced around underneath the bridge. The bullet shattered a rock next to Leon's feet. She opened her eyes and took a step back, covering her ears.

"What the hell?!" All hope for a calm discussion had disintegrated with that rock.

She needed to pull it together for Oliver. For Jon.

She walked a few steps towards him and stopped. She brought her other hand up to help steady the gun. He was halfway into the van and reaching into his pocket for his keys when she pointed the gun at the biggest part of him and pulled the trigger again. His body lurched forward from the impact. He clutched his stomach with his hands as blood trickled down his shirt.

"You BITCH!" He screamed at her and fumbled with the keys in his pocket.

Rebecca's hands were shaking as she took a deep breath and fired again. The bullet hit the metal door to his van with a clank and ricocheted off into the dirt. He dove to the ground and dropped his keys in the dust around his feet. She might not be the best shot, but she was the most determined. She knew she wasn't walking away until she had some sort of justice for Oliver and Jon. As he bent down to get his keys, Rebecca closed the distance between them and planted herself just out of arm's reach. When Leon collected his keys and raised his head, he was staring down the barrel of her gun.

He held his hands in front of his face, "No! Please, I'm not who you think I am! Noooo…" She fired the gun again, cutting his cries short. The bullet tracked through his right palm and entered his forehead, an inch below his hairline. For a few seconds he stood there, oblivious to what had happened. Leon looked at her and frowned, blinking as the dripping blood began to blur his vision. He reached out to her, his hands covered in the deep red fluid. For the first time, he noticed his palm, disintegrated by the bullet. He turned his hand over and saw through the middle of it down to the ground where his keys sat on the gravel, perfectly framed by the shredded skin around the hole in his palm.

Rebecca took a step back as Leon fell forward onto the dirt, covering up the keys he had tried so desperately to retrieve. His chest heaved as he clutched the dirt around him and moaned.

She stood over him as he bled onto the dirt and gravel, his brown hair stained black and matted around the wound at the back of his head. The gun slipped from her hand and fell, hitting the ground with a heavy thud and settling onto the loose dirt not far from her feet. She jumped back, as if it were a thing to be afraid of. She stood there trembling, arms limp at her sides and eyes wide with fright. A large truck rumbled overhead, bringing her focus back to where she was, and what she had done.

Rebecca bent down to retrieve the gun and ran back to her car. She knew she needed to get out of there, and fast. There had been a lot of shots fired. Was it three, or four? She couldn't remember. It had all happened so quickly. She threw herself into her car and slammed the door, throwing it into reverse to turn back around towards the road without stopping to put her seatbelt on. Gunning the gas as hard as she could, her tires spun dirt over Leon as she flew up the feeder towards the highway. Once there, she glanced at herself in the rear-view mirror. Almost unrecognizable, she wondered when she had turned into this wild-eyed woman. She was Rebecca, calm and cool and focused. She didn't get emotional and she certainly didn't kill people. She wasn't positive she believed in a god, or karma, or whatever... but she was certain whoever or whatever would understand why she had done this. An eye for an eye, right?

Rebecca slowed to the speed limit, aware she was going about twenty miles per hour over it. That was the last thing she needed right then, to get pulled over by a cop. She smirked at the irony. She was afraid they would finally do their job and pull her over, as she was leaving a place where she had to do their job for them. *C'est la vie.*

Her hands had finally stopped shaking by the time

she turned onto her road. Polly, the young single mother who lived a few houses down, was mowing her front yard. Polly looked up as she approached and waved to her. Rebecca returned the greeting before she realized what she was doing. Her car window was still down and she caught the scent of cut grass and the putter of a lawn mower as she drove past. A few more houses down, there were Andrew and Paul, having a glass of iced tea on their front porch. They also waved to Rebecca. She waved back to them. Can't be rude, can't be weird, can't let anyone suspect she was anything but poor grieving Rebecca.

Finally at her driveway, she pulled into her garage and let the door close behind her. She sat in her car, hands still on the wheel, staring ahead at the unpainted sheet rock wall of her garage. She just killed someone. He deserved it… but she had taken a life. She should feel... something. Remorse. Guilt. Fear. But she didn't. She didn't feel anything at all.

She was tired. So very tired. She stepped through the small door into the kitchen, tossed her keys on the counter, and shuffled towards her bedroom.

It was still weird, being in there without him. Without even the scent of him anymore. Everything was fading so fast. With her clothes and shoes still on, she climbed onto their bed and moved over to his side. She clutched his pillow and buried her face in it, trying to feel him one more time. She was asleep within minutes.

***

She woke the next morning to a bright room, the light she hadn't turned off last night glared down at her. As Rebecca leaned over to kick her shoes off, she noticed dust on her comforter. The dust she had carried into her home on her shoes, from that ground by the canal where she killed a man. She killed him. Shaking off the memory, Rebecca pulled her legs out of her jeans and slipped into her favorite pajama pants. She wasn't planning on leaving the house that day, so she might as well be comfortable. She and Jon started every morning with a cup of coffee and that day was no different, except she finally felt like she could grieve in peace. She could think about her sweet boy and her missing husband and all the good things that they were. Finally knowing what had happened to Jon, she was no longer burdened with the unknown, with the realization that a killer was out there who was connected to her in the most intimate way. She had taken care of that. She sat in the kitchen while the coffee dripped into the pot, its strong aroma filling the small space. Walking with her cup into the living room, she settled onto the couch and turned on the TV.

The volume kicked on before the black screen dissolved into a picture, so she knew it was Amy Andrews before she saw the flaming red hair and tight black dress. She used to have a dress like that, before pregnancy ruined her svelte figure and she was stuck wearing 'mom' jeans for the rest of her life. Rebecca twirled a few strands of her straight brown hair around her finger. She should dye it red. Jon always joked that he wanted a redhead. Rebecca leaned back against the couch pillows and sipped her coffee as Amy reported on the latest news.

"... his body was found early this morning by local fishermen. Several bullet wounds indicate the cause of death, but the question remains: Why was Leon Phillips shot? Sources reveal nothing appeared to have been stolen. His wallet was still in his pocket, full of cash and credit cards. This is the exact same location as another mystery – a month back four-year-old Oliver Crow drowned here in his father's car. His father, Jon Crow remains missing. Could this latest incident be related?

Rebecca turned the channel, unable to see Oliver's face plastered all over the TV yet again. She wished they would stop doing that: some people were trying to grieve in peace. The next station was also reporting on Leon, but thankfully they had left the Crows out of it or had already shown their faces.

Most of it was standard news fare, after the shooting incident, anyway. Tide reports, hurricane outlooks, and more hot weather. Always with the hot weather. If she wasn't so attached to their home, and the memories there, she would move somewhere cold. Somewhere that actually had all four seasons, not the unbearably long summers they had there on the Texas coast.

Rebecca was pouring her second cup of coffee in the kitchen when she heard a new report faintly from the living room.

"Leon Phillips was only in town for the week to visit family before he headed back to Florida. His mother said this was his first trip to Texas, and unfortunately this was also his last. Signing out, this is..."

Coffee fell onto her hand as it overflowed the cup. She dropped the pot onto the counter and ran into the living room. The current station had already moved onto something else so she frantically switched channels, looking for someone still covering the story. She made it back around to Amy Andrews as they took a break to talk about traffic.

Rebecca screamed at the TV, "Are you serious? No one cares about that right now!" She held her breath while they talked about another back-up on Highway 288, and more construction on I-10.

Amy finally came back on and confirmed what the other station had said. Leon Phillips was only in town that week. He couldn't have killed Jon and Oliver. He was in

Florida a month before, not under a bridge by a canal in Texas. She sank to the floor as a whimper escaped her lips.

She had killed an innocent man.

She, Rebecca, had killed someone who had nothing at all to do with Jon and Oliver. He really was just a nice guy who was trying to help her out. That wasn't how it was supposed to turn out. She was supposed to get justice and peace. She just wanted to be able to move on with her life. But she was a murderer, and the real killer was still out there.

16

Captain D's was a neighborhood institution, and Tommy and James' second favorite place to grab lunch. Their first was the Mexican Meat Market, but that was on the other side of town and they were in a hurry. D's was shaped like a boat, or maybe it had been an actual boat. James could never tell. Sun-bleached oyster shells filled the previously grassy bits between the parking lot and the building. They must have saved a fortune on mowing. There was the obligatory thick rope following the walkway from the parking lot to the front door, a staple for every seafood restaurant. But you didn't dare run your hand along it as you walked: the hardened rope fibers would poke the hell out of you. The main door had a boat wheel stuck to the front, and a porthole peeking out from the middle of that. Inside, a U-shaped bar filled the small space, and customers sat around it on uneven bar stools, watching their lunch get shucked right in front of them.

In the fall and winter, they liked the ice-cold oysters on the half shell. The flabby gray bits sitting in the palm of their shells didn't look appetizing, but a bit of horseradish and a dash of hot sauce would make it just right. Tommy liked his on a cracker, but James sucked his right out of the shell. In the summer, they took their oysters Rockefeller or fried. James was the sort to take risks, but even he didn't dare eat them raw in the off season. The warm waters off the Gulf of Mexico encouraged all sorts of bacteria to bloom and grow in the summers, and eating bad oysters was high on his list of things he never wanted to do.

Tommy was already there, with a plate of Rockefeller and fries in front of him, when James arrived. He swiveled a bar stool around and eased into it. "What, you don't wait for me?"

"You're late, and you know I gotta get back to the shop by twelve." Tommy kept his eyes on the plate he was inhaling.

"Screw 'em, they won't fire you for being late one day. You're the best mechanic they got."

Tommy nodded his agreement while chewing. He *was* the best mechanic, and he knew it. "I ordered you the fried basket and tea."

"I hope you're paying, I ain't got shit." Tommy always paid, but it was a fun little ritual to at least claim it was a surprise.

"Yeah I'll spot you, but you know rent is due in three days. Am I pickin' up your end again?" Tommy glanced at James, gulped another bite down, and took a few swigs of his tea.

"Yeah, I'll pay you back," James answered, though they both knew it was a lie.

Tommy had been paying both halves of the rent for the past three months, and James knew he'd keep doing it as long as James kept hanging out with him. No matter how mean or cranky James could be, Tommy was always there. He didn't know why Tommy stuck around, but he was glad he did. It meant the rent got paid, and most of his lunches were free. He was an all-right guy otherwise. Kind of funny, and super smart. Not as smart as James, of course, but right up there. He didn't have many friends, he was kinda quiet, and a lot of people thought he was weird. He was, but a lot of people also thought it.

Tommy took another bite and mumbled around his food, "Hey did you hear about that guy over in The Quarters? His girlfriend found him dead in their kitchen." He swallowed and motioned to the bartender to refill his sweet tea.

"Yeah, Martin." James looked down at the plate of food the bartender placed in front of him. "Can I get some cocktail sauce?"

"Oh yeah, doesn't your mom rent from him or somethin'?"

"Not anymore." James winked at him.

"You didn't..." He put his glass of tea down and sighed, "Damnit James, did you do somethin'?"

James paused with his fry in midair and stared at Tommy, his eyes narrow and his jaw tight. "So what if I did?"

Tommy shook his head and wiped his hands on his napkin. He avoided James' glare as he pulled out his wallet and tossed a twenty and a five on the counter. "I gotta get back, see you later."

"I might be late, I got some shit to take care of."

Tommy nodded and quickly left the restaurant. James didn't care. If anything he was glad Tommy was gone. He had a headache coming on and the little shit always annoyed him when he had a headache. James rubbed his temples and looked at the money on the table, contemplating pocketing it. The bartender was faster, and before James could decide, he had swiped it off the table and stuck it in the cash register, smiling at James.

"Whatever, I'm done anyway," James mumbled as he stood up to leave.

As he stepped out of Captain D's, he saw two missed calls from his mama. She had probably heard about Martin; she never missed any of the local gossip. James readied himself for an endless stream of chatter and dialed her number.

"Hey mama, sorry I missed you. What's up?"

"Jimbo – you're never gonna believe this! Miz Hopper said that her neighbor, Beatrice, was walkin' down

Pence St. yesterday and saw all sorts of flashin' cars in front of Martin's house! She tried to get close to see what was goin' on but the cops made her stay back. Anyway, she saw them bring out someone in a body bag and you're never gonna guess who it was! It was Martin! Hot damn, how's that for getting' out of payin' rent this month? I mean, I should feel bad that he died, but I really don't, that shrimp was an asshole. So I guess…"

James climbed into his van and set the phone down on the passenger seat while he started the engine and turned the radio off. He pulled out onto the highway before picking the phone back up.

"…gonna go down to the bingo hall now that I have some extra money since I don't have to pay rent this month. Can you believe they serve beer down there now? Hot damn Imma play bingo and drink some beer. They just opened a new room in the back for those casino games and they're not supposed to pay real money 'cause it's illegal but…"

"Hey mama I gotta go, I'll stop by this weekend, okay?"

"Okay honey, you be careful now and tell Tommy I said hello! He needs to come see…"

"Mama, I gotta go. Love you, bye." He could still hear her talking as he hung up the phone.

That woman could ramble for days if you didn't stop her, and he wasn't in the mood to listen to it. He had a raging headache, and needed to figure out how to make some money quick. He could probably get his job back at the shop, he was pretty sure Tommy could talk Trey into it, but he didn't want to work there anyway. They started way too early in the morning and expected you to stay there all fucking day, only giving you thirty minutes for lunch. Shit, he almost had a heat stroke under some old dude's F250 a month ago and the boss man didn't give a shit at all, he just asked if he was done changing the oil. James could do a lot better than that dump.

He drove east along Galveston's Seawall Boulevard, cruising slowly behind the heavy traffic. Gulls cawed to each other, and waves crashed against the sand below the road. The water was kept at a distance, separated from the cars by a concrete wall about five feet higher than the shore. It was far enough back from the tide, though. The water didn't usually lick the concrete unless it was hurricane season and they had a good one coming. Then, despite warnings, surfers would dot the water as far as you could see, sitting on their boards with leashes tied to their ankles, and waiting for the heavy waves. They would come down from as far as San Antonio, Dallas even. James didn't see any surfers that day, though. The waves were nothing but mush and shore breakers. It didn't matter anyway, surfers didn't leave empty cars full of cash parked on the beach, waiting for them to return from the water. They arrived on foot, having walked from a nearby hotel if they traveled, or their house if they were a local. If they did drive, it was never anything worth breaking into.

There was finally a break in traffic, and James gunned it towards the jetties, not really sure what he wanted to do but knowing he needed to do something, and soon. He scanned the cars parked along the side of the road and in the shop parking lots on his left. Too many people. He needed to get away from all of those damn people.

He slowed down as he pulled into the parking lot of the East side jetties. It was a good spot to get away from people for a minute. Hopping down from the driver's seat, James went around to the side of the van and opened the sliding door. That's where he kept his cooler, always with a couple of beers in it. They weren't as cold as they were yesterday, the ice had melted, and he didn't think to pick up any more, but it was better than nothing. James grabbed a can of lukewarm beer and tossed a handful of aspirin in his mouth before taking a long chug.

It was only a hangover, but it was a doozy. He and Tommy had put a lot back the night before, sitting on their balcony and watching the tourists. Fucking Tommy took off to bed early like a little bitch, but James had stayed there drinking until the ink black sky above him broke with the gray haze of an impending sunrise.

There was just one other car in the jetty parking lot, a sweet little red sportster parked in the far corner closest to the water. James sat on the open door frame and drank the rest of the beer. The only breeze, coming off the gulf, was full of steam and heat. Nothing could cool you down when the weather was like that. Warm, salty air pricked the taste buds on his tongue and the smell of fish wafted in from the west. The shrimp boats were probably docked somewhere, unloading their catch.

He squinted against the bright sun and raised his hand to his eyes, trying to focus. It looked like someone was fishing down at the very end of the jetties. Not uncommon, but it was uncommon for him to be the only one out there. It was usually packed with fishermen... witnesses. The red car must be his, but someone with that nice of a car usually didn't spend their days fishing. He was probably a weekender trying to be 'one with nature' or some shit. James opened another beer and watched the man. It didn't look like he was catching much. But a guy like that, he probably had some serious cash on him. James chugged the rest of the beer, tossed the can in the sand on the side of the parking lot, and reached into the back seat of the van to grab his pistol. He chuckled to himself, remembering Peter's line from The Godfather, "Leave the gun, take the Cannoli." Except for James, it was "Leave the beer, take the gun." The van doors closed with a thud as he turned towards the jetties, sliding the gun into the back of his waistband.

He stepped carefully between the smooth, massive gray rocks that made up the jetties. The rocks were tinged with pink striations and were worn smooth on the edges from years of crashing waves. The large boulders were placed as close together as possible, but the seams could be a foot across in some places. More than one person had broken an ankle not paying attention. The pile of rocks jutted far out into the water. Waves crashed against them on the public beach side while slightly calmer waters lapped the other. That was the side the barges went down on their way inland. There was another jetty that made up the other side of the canal, but it wasn't open to the public. James had only been on it a couple of times at night. It wasn't set up for fishing, and the gaps between the rocks were wide enough for a man to fall down. He kept walking, keeping his eyes on the cracks and the fisherman. The man glanced up at him once, then ignored him as he got a pull on his line. He wore a brand-new fishing shirt, the slit in the back waved at James in the breeze and he wouldn't have been surprised if a price tag had popped out of it, still attached. The man's jeans were spotless, and a dark deep blue that hadn't seen many washings. He had on loafers with barely a scuff on them. Stuck to the top of his head, probably hiding a bald spot, was a tan, brimmed hat. James was just a few feet away by the time the man looked back up. The sun had taken its toll on his pale face where pink swashes of sunburn flicked across his nose and licked the back of his neck.

"Hey there, catch anything?" James smiled at the stranger.

"Nah, but it's good just to be out here away from the office, you know?"

"Oh yeah, tell me about it. I've been working all

week. Fucking deadlines, you know?"

The man's eyes swept down James' stained shirt and worn jeans, traveling back up to take in his three-day-old stubble and bloodshot eyes. "Yeah, fuck 'em." He started to pack up his gear, his voice catching as he dismantled his poles. "Well I gotta get back, the old lady is waiting on me."

James knew he'd been caught in the lie, and that he made the stranger nervous. He seemed to have that effect on people, especially lately. Not that he gave a fuck. It just meant more people left him alone and he was all for that. But he wasn't letting that one get away, that guy definitely had some cash on him.

"Here, let me help you." James reached down and grabbed the pearl handled knife sitting on the rock by the man's ice chest. He opened and closed it almost absent-mindedly, grinning. The fisherman's eyes darted between James' face and the sharp blade. Finally, James left the knife open and gestured with it towards the man.

"Look, just give me your wallet and there won't be any trouble." That was a lie, but it was easier to be handed the wallet, than try to get it out of a dead man's back pocket later.

He thought the man was going to piss himself as he fumbled around in the back pocket of his designer jeans.

"Also... give me your watch too, and that ring."

It was going to be the easiest cash he'd made all week. And the guy looked like he'd have way more than thirty-two dollars on him. Screw that fat ass soccer dad and his whiny little kid.

James watched as the wallet slipped out of the man's sweaty hands and dropped to the ground. He rolled his eyes and gestured towards it with the knife, "Well, pick it up."

The fisherman reached down to pick up the wallet with shaking hands, keeping his head low so he wouldn't have to look at James. It was the perfect opportunity, James couldn't have written it better if it were a script.

James stepped forward and plunged the knife into the pink skin at the back of the guy's neck.

It went in easier than he would have thought, slicing the skin smoothly, only stopping once it hit bone. Blood shot out from around the knife, and the man fell forward onto the rocks. James sidestepped him to avoid getting blood on his shoes, and leaned down to retrieve the wallet, splattered with blood. He opened it and whistled low. "I knew it. I knew you'd have more than thirty-two dollars and dammit if you didn't come through!" He held four crisp one hundred dollar bills in his hand and grinned at the gasping man, now crouched down on the rocks. The stranger was going to die, there was no doubt about that.

James looked down the jetties and couldn't believe his luck. No one had pulled up in a car or walked down from the other part of the beach. The only other body he could see was a German Shepherd running along the sand, barking at the tide about a half a mile away. But usually where there was a dog, there was a person.

The man was gasping for breath, each one raspy and shallow.

James needed to clean up the mess, and fast.

He tossed the fishing gear into the churning water where the waves met the rocks. The poles and lures bobbed on the surface while the heavier weights and tackle box quickly sank below. James glanced one more time back at the dog. Still no person in sight. He leaned down and wiped the knife off on the man's jeans before closing it and sticking it in his pocket. James then pushed the man over the edge of the rocks, after he took his fancy watch, of course. He watched as the body tumbled down into the water. The fisherman landed face up and was pulled into the rolling foam, his eyes wide. That would chum up the waters real good for the next guy; you could get some good sized sharks to come around with that kind of bait.

James walked back to his van, whistling as he tossed the man's empty wallet into the water. Things were looking up. Maybe tomorrow, he'd buy Tommy's lunch for once.

17

Rebecca dug through her kitchen cabinets in a feeble attempt to find a lunch bag. She knew exactly where one was but couldn't bring herself to use the bright orange and blue striped bag with 'Oliver' embroidered in green on the flap. She bought it last Spring from the engraving kiosk at the mall. He had been ecstatic to see it, squealing with delight and immediately taking it to his room to fill with plastic dinosaurs and blocks. Never mind that it was for his lunch, Oliver was never one to pay attention to details.

No, she couldn't use his. Not yet.

Probably not ever.

Her thighs burned from crouching down to see into the cabinets. She gave up and sat on the kitchen floor. In front of her was another packed cabinet, filled with twenty different types of pots, assorted lids that never seemed to fit anything, and dust covered bowls. It wasn't a cabinet she visited often. The entire kitchen had been neglected as of late, except for the coffee pot. She was getting by on fast food and frozen pizzas when she did eat, which wasn't often.

Rebecca's air conditioner sputtered as it struggled to keep up with the summer heat. The humidity was especially high that day, and the thick wetness was suffocating, every breath a heavy draw. Opening a window for fresh air was out of the question, there was no fresh air to be had. It had all flown north for the summer. Wearing shorts and a tank top to stay cool, she could feel the crisp hardness of the tile floor on her exposed thighs. Rebecca wanted to sit there forever.

She leaned back against the cabinet and closed her eyes. An innocent man had died. A man with probably a wife, or a kid, or some kind of family, who were going through exactly what she was going through. Because of her, their nightmares had come true.

She ached for Jon and Oliver, and when she thought too long about that ache, she had to force herself to let her body breathe in and out, to eat, and to sleep. Every day it was harder, she was drowning in grief. She wondered if at some point she just wouldn't be able to pull all that off and her body would simply stop. That wouldn't be so bad; at least then she wouldn't have to miss them so damn much. But not that day. That day she had a reason to keep breathing. It was awful, what she had done to the man who was innocent. But the other guy was still out there, somewhere. And that wasn't okay, there should be consequences. Next time she'd just have to be sure he was the right one.

Her thighs peeled off the floor with a light smack as she stood up. There was a pile of reusable shopping bags somewhere. Jon had brought them home a few months ago trying to reduce their 'footprint', but they always forgot to grab them. She rummaged through the back of the pantry and finally found them shoved into the back corner. She grabbed a dark blue bag embossed with whales and filled it with two bottles of water and the peanut butter and jelly sandwich that she had made earlier. Last time, sitting under that bridge for hours, she had grown hot, thirsty, and light-headed. This time she would be better prepared. Water, check. Sandwich, check. Gun, bullets... check. Sanity, well she could check that one off after tonight. It was the world's worst shopping list.

It was ridiculous, she knew that. But she didn't know how to function without her boys or her work. She only knew that it wasn't fair, and that someone needed to pay. At the very least, it gave her a reason to get out of bed.

She locked the door behind her and rushed down the sidewalk before stopping herself. She needed to act normal, calm. A quick glance down the street showed empty front porches and mostly empty driveways. No one was watching her, or accusing her of killing anyone. They were all living their normal lives.

Rebecca was in her car and driving down the highway when her dad called.

"Hey Becca, how are you?"

"I'm all right." She couldn't exactly say, 'I killed an innocent man the other day, but it's okay, because I'll get the right one this time.' He wouldn't understand and worse, he'd try to talk her out of it.

"I was thinking of coming down there, is this weekend a good time?"

She hesitated, "I'll let you know, okay?" That was the last thing she needed.

"Okay, well don't be a stranger. I'm here for you, you know that, right?"

"Yeah, okay. Hey, I gotta go." She hung up the phone before he could respond.

The bridge was coming up, but she couldn't go back there. Too risky. She drove over it, taking in the view from the top. That was always her favorite part of driving to the beach. Miles of coastline stretched out on each side and the blue horizon curved as far as she could see. The water blended from a dark blue to a light blue-green, punctuated by white frothy breaks. Beneath her, barges and small boats lay scattered across the canal.

The bridge ended at an intersection with roads on either side, and the beach straight ahead. She felt pulled to the water and headed that way. She weaved around the summer crowds and scanned for a quiet place to stop and think. The crowds thinned as she made her way further down, and she could see the jetties in the distance. A dog ran across them, barking and chasing seagulls.

As she drove closer, she noticed a white van pulling out of the jetty parking lot. It was old, like Jon had said. Rust patches marred the dull white surface, and the back doors hung crooked on their hinges. Rebecca's heart seized up, forgetting how to beat. She turned off the radio, spinning the dial so hard it wouldn't have surprised her if it had broken off in her hand. At the next intersection, she turned left to follow him. Unable to see the driver, she kept a few cars between them so he wouldn't notice her. When he turned onto the bridge and headed north, she was still behind him, unable to believe her luck in finding him so fast. She just needed to figure out what to do once she did catch up with him.

Rebecca glanced in the rear-view mirror at the booster seat behind her. "We got him, Ollie. We got him." Oliver laughed that sweet belly laugh of his and smiled at her, his eyes twinkling. When she looked back towards the road in front of her, she couldn't see the van.

"Okay Rebecca, it's okay. He's probably on the other side of the bridge, you'll see him when you hit the top." She muttered to herself. A quick peek at the rear-view mirror showed an empty booster seat.

The van was nowhere in sight when she hit the peak of the bridge. As she descended, she looked around, hoping to see him parked at the bait shop, or at the edge of the water. Nothing.

"Shit!" She slammed her hand on the steering wheel, hard enough to press the horn in. A woman driving a small yellow car in the lane next to her cast her a questioning look. "Sorry, not you."

In the sea of tail-lights in front of her, she thought she could see the rear of the van again. But, by the time she was able to get close enough, she could tell it wasn't the same van. Emblazoned across the side in a swoosh of red and blue paint were the words: 'Paulie's Electric'. No rust.

Undefeated, Rebecca continued driving. Every intersection was a possibility, and every red light a nuisance. She retraced her route to the beach, the jetties, the bridge. The view was magnificent from the top at that time of day, the setting sun threw oranges and reds across the sky, reflecting in the water below. But Rebecca just glanced at it, her eyes still frantically searching. A few hours later she finally caught a break.

Just off the highway, parked to the side of the Lucky S just ahead of her and on the right, was an old white van. Rebecca pulled up to the left of the van and put her car in park. It wasn't 'Paulie's Electric' or anyone else's 'Plumbing' or 'Air Conditioning' van. It was plain white, rusty in spots. It was him, she could feel it in her soul. Her keys clattered in her trembling hand as she realized the driver was still in the van and about to open the door. He would have to walk right by her car to go in the store. She sank down into her seat and held her breath, hoping to hide behind the tinted windows of her car.

The man got out and shut his door with a muffled thud. He shuffled past her car, a few feet from where she was sitting. He looked tired, but she could understand that. She knew what it was like to live with the crushing guilt of killing someone innocent. Not that she could call what she was doing 'living'. It didn't matter, none of that mattered. She just needed to make it right, then she could figure out how to live with herself.

He limped as he walked toward the doors to the gas station. His dark skin was weather worn, and his clothes hung off his thin frame as if he had lost forty pounds since he bought them. He carried a red plastic gas can in one hand, and a handful of keys in the other. As he walked away she noticed a bulge at the back of his shirt near his waist. That was it. That was the gun he used on Jon. She was sure of it.

18

"Hey, are you still in town? Looks like the AAA guy is here already, we'll just ride with him. You can meet us at the mechanic shop, it's closer to home anyway."

"I'm not, but I can turn around. They got there fast."

"Yeah, I thought so too. But he's not in a tow truck. This is probably the car service so we don't have to ride with the tow guy. Either way, they really need to invest in nicer vehicles. This van looks like it's about to fall apart. I'll call you back when we're on the road again. Love you."

Jon hung up the phone as the rusty white van pulled up behind his car and stopped a few feet away. He leaned into the open window of the Chevy and held out his phone to Oliver.

"Here buddy, play your games for a bit. Daddy's gonna talk to this guy for a minute."

Oliver eagerly grabbed it, grinning from ear to ear.

Jon smiled an identical, ear-to-ear, grin. A son and father had never looked more alike than Ollie and Jon. Same curly blond hair, always shaggy and full of cow-licks. Same bright blue eyes, always twinkling at a joke no one else had heard. They even had identical dimples when they smiled, only on the left side.

As Jon straightened and turned to face the AAA van, he noticed the driver was already walking towards him. He was a middle-aged man, not unlike Jon himself. He wore an over-sized fishing shirt and a hat with a couple of hooks dangling from the brim. It was hard to tell how old he was; the sun could age you faster than time ever would. The man's dark brown skin was rough and dry, thick from too much time outside. Slightly shorter than Jon, he probably would have been taller if he had better posture. The man swayed as he walked, slightly hunched over, doing the best he could with the leg he was given. Jon couldn't tell what exactly was wrong with it, but the man could barely put any weight on his right leg before swinging the other one around in an almost comedic rhythm.

"Hey there! I'm Jon Crow," Jon jogged forward a few steps and met the man halfway.

The man held Jon's outstretched hand like a dead fish, shook it up and down a few times and, to Jon's relief, finally let go. "Hi. Arthur Washington. You havin' trouble?"

"Yeah, just a flat tire though. You're with AAA?"

"What? No, I was headin' home when I saw you guys pulled over here and thought you might need some help. Were ya'll just at the beach? I thought I remembered seein' your car and your little boy." The man peered around Jon, searching for Oliver.

Jon tilted his head to the side, "Oh well, you didn't have to trouble yourself. We have help coming, they should be here any minute now."

Arthur's face fell as he mumbled, "Oh, okay." He took a few steps towards his van and looked down the highway before he stopped. "Hey. You got a light? I can't find my damn lighter and I've been wantin' a cigarette all day." He pulled a pack from the front pocket of his shirt and opened it. His leathery hands fumbled with the thin cigarettes, and one of them fell to the ground at his feet.

"I'll get that for you," Jon said as he reached down to pick up the dusty cigarette. He felt sorry for the man. It was obvious that Arthur had money problems. His van had rust holes as big as a fist, and his clothes looked like they had been bought for someone else, someone a lot larger. He probably picked them up at Goodwill. With Jon's face close to the ground, he got a good look at the man's feet. A big toe was poking out of a hole in one of his mottled blue house shoes that had long ago lost their fuzz.

Jon's fingertips had just wrapped around the cigarette when a blinding pain exploded at the back of his head. As he fell to the ground, the cigarette rolled out of his hand and back onto the dust. Jon's mouth gaped like a fish thrown onto the banks, and for a minute he thought he was going to suffocate there with his face in the dirt. He pushed up from the ground with a gasp, and his hand went to the back of his head. When he pulled it back, wet sticky blood coated his fingertips. Nausea overcame him and he fell to his hands and knees, throwing up the lunch he had just eaten.

Another explosion erupted at the base of his skull, harder and more intentional than the last.

His arms crumpled beneath his body and he fell into his own vomit, puffing up small clouds of dust and wet, half-digested bits of food. He didn't touch his wound again, and he didn't see his fingertips coated with more blood. His eyes forever focused on the left rear tire of his car, and he lay still while a small puddle of urine pooled around him.

Arthur dropped the blood-stained rock to the ground with a thud and shuffled to the side of the Chevy.

"Hey little guy, your dad wanted me to get you out of the car. What's your name?"

Oliver looked around the man but couldn't see his dad. He cocked his head to the left, taking in the stranger. "Oliver," he whispered.

"Oliver! What a great name, Oliver. Come on now, son, and let's get you out of this seat." He started unbuckling the straps that held Ollie into his car seat. When he was free, the man reached under his arms and lifted him out. He wrapped his hands around Oliver, pressing his small frail frame against his own chest. The man's eyes closed and his breath quickened. He couldn't believe his luck. But he was pressing a little too hard, and Oliver started to squirm away. He tried to hold onto him, but he wasn't as quick as he used to be. Oliver slipped to the ground and skittered away from the man with a suspicious look.

"Come on now boy, let's get you into the van and everything will be all right." He took a step forward, swinging his good leg around to gain momentum.

Oliver kept his eyes on the stranger and walked backwards around the rear of the car, his small hand grasping at the blue Chevy as he went. His foot caught on something and he fell, scraping his hands in the dirt. His lips quivered as he stared for a minute at his stinging palms. When he looked around to see what he had tripped over, he began to scream.

"Daddy? Daddy!?" He moved up to his dad's side and grabbed his arm, shaking him as hard as he could. "Daddy!"

The man reached down to grab him by the arm, but Oliver jerked away and ran as fast as he could. Away from his father and the only safe thing he knew, away from the car and his games and songs, and away from the strange man. He came to a halt at the edge of the bank, a few inches from falling in. Looking over his shoulder, he saw the man inching towards him with his hands held out.

"Hey little man, I'm not gonna hurt you. It's okay. We'll get your dad to the hospital, they'll make him all better. I already called the ambulance, but first you gotta come with me."

Oliver hesitated, confusion sweeping over him. Tears sprang to his eyes as he looked around the man to see his dad laying there on the ground, so still and quiet. Maybe he was sleeping. Sometimes it was hard to wake his dad up, but there was blood on his head, his hands, and the ground, and that didn't look right to Oliver. He knew what blood was, he had cut his arm last month when he fell off the swing at Riley Park. His dad had cleaned him up at the water fountain and gotten a bandage from his car. Oliver knew where his dad kept the bandages, in a first aid kit in the trunk, but he didn't know how to open the trunk. Besides, the strange man was still looking at him funny and getting closer.

The tips of the man's outstretched hands had barely brushed Oliver when he jerked away. He stumbled and tottered on the edge of bank, arms flailing to find balance. But it was too late, momentum had already taken over, and had pulled him over the edge and into the water. Yelping, he leaned forward as he fell, but the sounds were cut off with a loud crack as his forehead knocked against the edge of the concrete embankment. His body eased into the water with only a gentle splash echoing back to the man standing above him.

Frantic, Arthur knelt and waved his arms around in the water, hoping to make contact with Oliver. He leaned over the concrete edge, one hand steadying himself while the other continued its blind search. His fingertips brushed against something silky and he immediately closed his fingers around it and jerked up as hard as he could. A fistful of sandy blond hair broke the surface, water glistening off the light locks, followed by Oliver's small head. A deep gash across his forehead dripped blood onto his face and into his eyes, but Oliver didn't seem to notice. He was so very still.

Arthur lifted him up out of the water and placed him on the sandy ground. Panic set in as he attempted CPR. He had no idea what he was doing, but knew it involved breathing into Oliver's mouth and pounding on his thin chest. Worried he would break his thin ribs, Arthur stopped and rocked back on his heels, watching for any signs of life.

Nothing. He leaned forward again, holding his hands together in a double fist and placed them on Oliver's chest. With hesitation, he pushed down a couple of times, then harder as he realized the little boy was still not breathing.

"Nooooo!" He had come so far and was so close.

The man fell back down next to Oliver's lifeless body and caressed his peaceful face. He was so beautiful, it was such a shame. An eighteen-wheeler rumbled overhead, interrupting his thoughts. He glanced at his watch and pulled himself up to his feet.

Arthur leaned down and put one arm under Oliver's neck and the other underneath his knobby knees. With a groan, he stood back up, cradling Oliver's small body against his chest. He lowered his face to the wet blond curls and exhaled, disappointed. He hadn't seen one as sweet as that in a long time.

The man reached the open back door of the car and placed Oliver into his booster seat. There was a blue stuffed elephant next to him, and Arthur picked it up and placed it on Oliver's lap. The air inside the car was still blowing cool, and the radio played faintly. The keys were still in the ignition. He closed the door and looked around, finally spotting the blood stained rock he had dropped earlier. He shuffled toward Jon's body, old joints screaming at him as he bent down to retrieve the rock.

Back at the car, he sat down in the driver's seat and placed it into drive. He eased out, left the heavy rock resting on the gas pedal, and closed the door behind him. The tires quietly crunched on the loose gravel and dirt as the car inched towards the water's edge. He was halfway to his van when the underside of the car scraped against the concrete embankment as it dropped into the water. It bobbed for a minute before sinking to the bottom.

He stopped at Jon's body, hunched over awkwardly

in the dirt. His wallet came out of his back pocket easy enough, Arthur wasn't leaving completely empty handed. He wasn't strong enough to lift him so he sat down on the ground beside him and pulled up his knees. As he straightened his legs, he pushed Jon's body towards the water with his feet. Roll after roll, inch by inch, he finally had him at the edge of the bank. Arthur looked down into the murky water but could only see bubbles where the car had gone in just minutes before. With one more kick, Jon tumbled into the water, following Oliver and his blue Chevy.

Arthur wiped his hands on his jeans and shuffled back to his van. He pulled back onto the highway, nervously glancing around, but no one was looking his way. He stepped on the gas and sped off into the night.

19

The bell over the door of the Lucky S jingled as the man made his way into the store. Rebecca peeked over the edge of her window and looked around the parking lot. Besides her and the van, there was only one other vehicle. A tall thin boy, no more than 18, was pumping gas into his truck. Laughter floated from the passenger seat as he leaned in to talk to someone Rebecca couldn't see. The truck's tank reached capacity with a short click, and the boy nestled the handle back into the holder. He returned to the driver's seat with a youthful hop, and pulled out of the parking lot.

Rebecca could see the man through the window as he said something to the cashier and pointed to the clear acrylic lottery ticket display sitting on the counter. Piled high with a variety of scratch-off games, ranging from $1 to $20, it blocked most of her view of the cashier. The man was still digging around in his wallet, so she slipped out of her car and closed the door behind her with a soft thud. Crouched low, she waddled to the front of her car to peek around the hood. He was still at the counter, putting change back into his wallet. She shuffled towards the far side of his van, hunched over and holding her breath. Rebecca tried the handle on the sliding door. Of course he hadn't locked it, he probably knew no one would want to steal anything from that piece of junk.

The faint tinkling of the door-bell reached her again when he left the store and walked toward the pumps with the red gas can dangling from his fingertips. She crept into his van and closed the door behind her, hoping there was enough distance between her and the pumps for him to not hear the click of the door as it latched. Crouched behind the driver's seat, sweat dripped into her eyes but she was too afraid to wipe them. Beneath her knees, she could see only the sandy floorboard littered with crumpled receipts, take-out containers, straw wrappers, unopened mail, a few tools shiny with oil and half wrapped in old rags, and a bright green lighter with a crooked sticker that said 'Buy your own fucking lighter'. Jon's gun, stashed against her back in the waistband of her jeans, dug into her skin as she waited for the man to return. She moved to pull it out when her eyes locked onto the discarded green lighter. An idea began to form, and she eased the gun out of its hiding spot.

Small rocks and dirt scattered beneath his feet as the man shuffled closer to the van. He opened the door and eased into the driver's seat, pushing the fabric back and into her. Rebecca held her breath. The man placed the gas can on the floor to her right, never noticing that she was only inches away. If he had stretched his hand out, his fingers would have touched her knee. But he didn't. He pulled his arm back to the front, and his keys rattled in his other hand, ready to start the van.

She pressed the barrel of the gun against the back of his neck and whispered, "Don't move."

The man gasped and tried to turn around to see what was happening. The keys slipped from his fingers and dropped to the floor.

"I said don't move!" Rebecca's voice shook with false confidence.

He faced forward and stared at the palm trees that lined the far edge of the parking lot. His voice quivered as he said, "Take whatever you want, just don't hurt me."

She climbed into the front passenger seat, keeping the gun pointed at him. For the first time since she spotted him, she was able to get a good long look at the man who took everything from her. He looked average enough. His dark brown skin was weather-worn from years of fishing or working outside, and remnants of curly black hair peeked out from beneath his ball cap. The whites of his eyes reflected the street light as he stared at the gun in her hands. He clasped his shaking hands tightly together in his lap. An acrid smell filled the van and Rebecca looked down to see a dark stain spreading between his legs. Disgusted, she waved the gun towards the back seat before she could lose her nerve.

"Move to the back. Now."

She coughed and covered her nose with the collar of her shirt as he moved past her to get into the back seat. She fought back a gag as he finally settled, and again pleaded, "Please take whatever you want. I ain't got much, but you can have it."

"Do you have any rope, or fishing line?"

His wide eyes darted around him as he stuttered, "Yeah, in the glove box. Over there." He pointed to the front of the van.

Rebecca's eyes narrowed, and she felt behind her for the glove box clasp. She wasn't about to turn her back on him. He was a tricky one, this old man. Like she would fall for that. She felt her way around the edges of the glove box and found the handle. She pulled it open and half turned to look inside. There was a small spool of rope, just like he said.

"Give me your pocket knife. I know you have one, everyone has one. And give me your gun, too."

"What gun? You can have my knife, here," he said as he awkwardly dug into his pocket and held up the closed knife with trembling hands.

Her face flushed with anger, "The gun at your back, I saw it earlier. Don't mess with me."

"I swear I don't have a gun, what are you talking about?"

"Behind you, I saw it when you walked into the store earlier. It's at your back, tucked into your waistband. Turn around!" It was all taking too long. She didn't care if she was caught, but she needed to make sure he paid for what he did first.

He turned and lifted up the back of his shirt to reveal... a rag. A formerly white rag, stained tan over the years and spotted with oil. Not a gun. Rebecca stared at the rag for a minute before pulling it from his waist and tossing it to the floor of the van. Whatever, so it wasn't a gun. That didn't mean he hadn't killed Jon and Oliver. He just hadn't used a gun. She had figured that much, anyway.

She set her gun down beside her and cut off a piece of rope, "Tie up your feet. Now."

His hands shook as he fumbled with the rope. Tears streamed down his face, cutting a river through the dust and dirt caked there. She cut off another piece and wiped the sweat off her forehead with the back of her arm.

She glanced out of the window. Another car had pulled up to the gas pumps, a blue Toyota. A short, chubby woman wearing a skirt suit stepped out and glanced around, as all women should do when alone in a dark place, before she slid her credit card into the machine. Rebecca stopped what she was doing, she didn't want any movement to catch the woman's eye. But of course they weren't visible. The woman was standing at the pumps, in the spotlight of a flickering yellow bulb. Rebecca and the man were in a dark van, in a darker corner of the parking lot.

He finally finished tying his feet together and she gave it a tug, satisfied it would hold.

"Hold out your arms"

"Please, please don't hurt me. I got a wife at home, and I got three kids. The youngest just started walking... please..."

"Shut up," She said as she tied his hands together with the piece of rope. Girl Scout, she was not, but she only needed him to lay still for a few minutes at least. Once she started, anyway.

"Now lay down on the seat," she said as she tucked her gun back into her waistband and reached for the can of gasoline. She stared at it in her hands, took a deep breath, and moved closer to him.

He looked from the gasoline to her, then back again to the gasoline. "Why are you doing this? I didn't do nothing to…"

"Shut. Up," she whispered, stuffing the oily rag into his mouth.

Rebecca hefted the gasoline can onto her lap and popped the pour spout open. The heavy can was full, and it didn't take much effort to spill some out onto his legs. It became a little lighter as she moved up his body, paying special attention to his chest. She figured that part would need more... since there was more body there to get rid of. She had never thought about it before, how much gasoline it would take to keep a body burning.

Reaching his head, she stopped and looked at him. His wide brown eyes pleaded with her and a whine escaped as he tried to cry out around the rag in his mouth. His body bucked on the seat. The old van reeked of gasoline and urine, both burning her eyes. Hurrying, she continued to pour the gasoline over his neck, then his arms, leaning on his chest to reach higher. There was still quite a bit left in the can, so she nestled it between his waist and the seat. She hoped it would continue the job from there. When she pulled away from him, her left arm was wet. She lifted it to her nose and inhaled the unmistakable scent of gasoline. Rebecca wiped at her arm with her hand and reminded herself to clean it better once she was home.

She retrieved the green lighter from the floorboards and flicked the small wheel. A bright orange flame danced in the dark backseat of the rickety white van. The man squirmed, and a muffled shout squeezed past the bits of rag.

"This is for Oliver and Jon, you sick bastard."

Rebecca touched the lighter to the edge of the oil rag hanging from his mouth and held it there as the flame crawled up the dirty cotton toward his face. His shrieks became louder, still muffled around the rag. She opened the sliding door of the van and put one leg out, hoping for a quick getaway. With the other, she steadied herself in her crouched position and leaned towards the man's pant legs with the lighter. The flame moved much quicker across his soaked jeans. So quick, she wasn't able to jump back in time as it rushed down his legs as it followed the trail of gasoline she had poured there. She was still leaning on the edge of the seat when the flame whooshed past, sending a searing pain through her left arm. She bit her lip and jumped from the van. Shoving the sliding door closed, not caring about the sound it made, she crouch-ran back to her car, holding her burned arm close to her chest.

Chest heaving as if she had run a marathon, Rebecca gasped for air. She was finally able to get the key into the ignition on the third try, around shaking hands and a pounding heart. The parking lot was empty. The blue Toyota had left, and she could see the clerk through the window of the store reading a magazine, oblivious to what was going on just a few feet away. She slammed the car into reverse and pulled out of the parking spot. The van beside her was filling up with bright orange and yellow flickers of light.

It was quite beautiful, the fire. It was mesmerizing, the way it danced and lit up the dark corner of the parking lot, everything a soft orange glow. But she didn't dare look at it in the rear-view mirror. She forced herself to keep her eyes forward, away from the fire, the mirror, and the possibility of seeing Oliver sitting there behind her again. He

148

would be scared; he wouldn't recognize the person she had become. She didn't recognize herself anymore.

A few miles later, she forced herself to slow down to the speed limit. Her heart raced when she saw flashing lights coming towards her on the highway. She gripped the steering wheel and kept her eyes forward as the police cruiser raced by her. Another wasn't far behind, and after that, a fire engine. She hoped they would be too late, that there wouldn't be much left of the man who had killed her family. He had gotten exactly what he deserved.

20

———

James left Tom's Pawn #2 on Downing Street exactly how he had gone in, with the dead fisherman's watch on his arm and the same four blood-smudged one-hundred dollar bills in his wallet. Not that they hadn't made him a good offer, they had. They had made a hell of an offer. But he kinda liked the watch, its black leather strap felt good on his wrist, smooth and sleek. His mama didn't need the money that month anyway, it's not like Martin was going to go around asking for it.

James kicked himself for not taking the man's credit cards before he threw the wallet into the water. There was probably a ton of credit on them. But, he reminded himself, credit cards are what got you in trouble. He was playing the long game. He needed to get enough to get his mama comfortable, then blow outta town. With that detective sniffing around, it was only a matter of time before they got wise to him. Shit, Detective Barnes would only need to visit Tommy once without James around to keep him in line, and he'd probably spill everything. Tommy was weak, and scared. James despised weakness but he made an exception for Tommy. Tommy paid the rent, bought most of their dinners, and didn't ask too many questions. But he was scared and, much like a dog, a scared man was a dangerous man.

James pulled up to the intersection of Wilkinson and Burbank, just four houses down from his mama's place. There was a Crown Vic parked along the side of the street. Through his open window he could tell the engine was off, but there was someone sitting in the driver's seat. The light turned green and James pulled forward, slower than he needed to, trying to get a glimpse of the driver as he passed the car. Cops were a rare sight in the Third. Most in the city had given up on them years ago, and that was all right with everyone who lived there. They had their own kind of justice, a street justice, and had always handled their own without any kind of outside help. Not that they never saw the red and blue lights, every now and then a rookie would roll in hoping to "clean up" their part of town. But they were met with a wall of silence, and witnesses always seemed to be out of town.

Detective Barnes waved to James as he came into sight. He was smiling that jackass confident smile of someone who knows they got you by the balls. James could play that game, too. He smiled and waved back, bringing the van to a stop and leaning over the passenger seat like he had all the time in the world.

"How's it going officer? Burnes, is it?"

Barnes shook his head, "Oh I'm good, just relaxing here for a minute. What're you up to? Coming to see your mama?"

James thought that was odd, why would the cops care about his mama?

"Yep, I gotta get, she's waiting on me."

"See you later, James," Detective Barnes said, not smiling this time.

James waved again as he pulled away, the fake smile on his face fading as he rolled out of sight. Goddamn nosy ass pigs. Well, as long as they were on his mama's street and not with Tommy, he was okay for now. Let him sit out there jacking off while he visited his mama. There wasn't anything illegal about visiting your mama on a Saturday afternoon.

He knocked on the door as he opened it. "Knock knock! It's me! Where are you?" He learned a long time ago to announce his presence; his mama liked to walk around in her drawers on laundry day and you never knew what day was laundry day.

"Hey baby! I'm back here! Give me a minute, I'll be right up," she called out from the back of the house.

James took a seat on the worn recliner; the same one his dad was sitting in the day he shot him. It had been reupholstered, of course, blood was hard to get out of fabric even if you treated it right away. Which they hadn't. The police had been there all evening asking their questions and taking pictures. It would have looked bad if his mama had stopped to spray 409 on the chair.

The living room was almost exactly how it had been all of James' life. His mama kept it decorated in broke-ass nouveau. An old entertainment center was the centerpiece, its drooping shelves covered in garage sale trinkets, yellowed school pictures of James, and an autographed replica of a race car. James couldn't identify which driver it was for; he was never a fan of NASCAR. It didn't make sense to him, to watch grown men drive in circles for hours. But his dad loved it and his mama had given him that signed car as a gift the Christmas before he died. His dad, of course, didn't care and complained about how much it probably cost, but it was one of the only things of his dad's that his mama had kept out on display. The TV was one James had given her last year. He found it in the back of someone's truck. It was a delivery truck parked behind the local Walmart, and he may or may not have waited for the driver to go inside before 'finding' a few TVs in the back. But it was real nice, a fifty-five incher. No cracks across that glass.

An old couch sat against the far wall, a worn afghan covering most of it. You could see hints of the brown and maroon floral design on the couch through the holes in the blanket. In front of the couch was a coffee table that you were never allowed to put your feet on. White doilies sat underneath candy dishes, inviting anyone to take a snack and stay a while. James leaned over to snag a mint from the candy dish as his mama walked into the room.

"Hey baby! Come hug my neck."

He popped the mint in his mouth and stood up to hug her, "Hey mama, you doing ok?" He tilted his head towards the back of the house.

"Oh yeah, just got a bit of a backup. The internets say I need to eat more fiber but that stuff is gross. You either mix it in some water and it's nasty, or you eat foods with a lotta fiber in it and *they're* nasty. Tastes like you're eatin' a handful of sand, if you ask me. I'll just take a little longer on the toilet, is all. But you didn't come here to hear about your mama's bowels. You hungry?"

"I'm really not, mama. And hey, I got you something." He changed the subject before she insisted on cooking for him. His stomach still remembered the last thing she'd made for him. That rotten mayo had messed him up for a while. He reached into his pocket and pulled out the cash.

"What is this, baby? I can't take your money, you work too hard for it. And besides, I told you I was fine." She pushed the money back towards him.

He held up his hands and stepped back. "Nope, I told you I was on to something good. This ain't nothing, mama. Really, I want you to have it. It would hurt my feelings if you didn't take it."

She counted the money in her hands before shoving it into her apron pocket. "This is great, baby. Thank you. Martin's mama took over his rent houses and now she thinks she's better than everybody. He's not even cold in his grave, and the damn bitch has gone and gotten all high-falootin'. But this'll shut her up for a while. I told her, I said, 'Maryanne now you know we been friends for a long time, how you gonna get hard with me on this?', but she don't care none.

She kicked that girl of his out of his house and guess what...
she's rentin' that one out too! And chargin' damn near an
arm and a leg, yeah she done lost her mind but this'll shut
her up for a little bit." She patted the apron pocket.

"What happened to your disability check?"

She wiped her nose with the back of her hand and
suddenly found the bottom of the coffee table extremely
interesting. "Well, I told you about the bingo hall?" Sandra
looked up at her son. "Joyce and I went down there last
week, back when we heard Martin had died, and played the
casino games in the back. I didn't think I had to pay my rent,
since he was dead and all... how was I supposed to know
Maryanne was gonna come knockin'? But Joyce heard from
Yolanda who heard from Yvette that this one machine was
payin' out real good so I played it all day and I was real far
ahead but then I started losin' and, well, you know how it
goes. Joyce won a hundred fifty on it, but that was as good
as we did."

James sighed. Just when he thought he was catching
her up, she did something to get behind again.

"It's all right, mama. I got you. When do you need
the rest of it?"

She moved to sit down at the kitchen table. "Next-
next Monday." She looked down at her hands and bit at the
edges of a hangnail on her thumb.

James went over to her and placed a hand on her
shoulder. "Mama, look at me. Mama, hey." He lifted her
chin. "Don't you worry, okay? You can count on me." He
leaned down and hugged her. "I got this, I'll call you in a few,
ok?"

He waved to Detective Barnes as he drove past on
his way back home, though the pig acted like he didn't see
him. Hell, James preferred it that way anyway. He should just
take care of the detective, but that for sure would rain down

a whole mess of attention he definitely didn't need. He didn't want anyone breathing down his neck while he tried to get the rest of his mama's rent money.

21

―――――

Even in between jobs, Fridays were still James' favorite day of the week. It was payday for the rest of the world... which meant payday for James. He just had to work a little differently to get his.

He and Tommy sat in the van watching blue collars come and go from Hurricane's Pub on Harborside Blvd. Galveston was not a beautiful island that day, the setting sun hid behind a gray wall and rain was pouring down in thick sheets. Rain was good if you were trying not to get a lot of attention. Nobody would notice a van with the engine on in the corner of a parking lot if they were running with their hoodie up and their head down. No one would later be able to describe you to an officer if they were hiding behind their umbrella. They had been there for about an hour, and not one of those coverall wearing jerks had so much as nodded in their direction. It was a busy day, all the rainy ones were. Shit, rain on a payday meant all the construction workers sent home on rain-outs went straight to the Pub where they started drinking at noon and didn't stop until the place closed down around them.

James leaned back in the driver's seat, arm casually draped on the center console. He could sit there for hours, watching people and listening to the rain hit the roof of the van. Tommy, on the other hand, couldn't sit still to save his life. That man was born twitching and hadn't stopped since. He was one of those nervous motherfuckers who always looked guilty of something. That didn't really help out James at the moment, considering they *were* guilty of a lot of things. He knew it was just a matter of time before Tommy lost his shit and went to the police, or they came to him. But he would have to deal with that later, when he wasn't worried about paying his mama's rent.

"James, we should go. There's too much heat on us right now anyway." Tommy glanced towards the driver's seat, avoiding eye contact.

"Calm down, I told you I just needed one more good hit. It's for my mama, you want to see her get kicked out on the street?"

"Of course not."

"Then shut up and – wait, look." James pointed to an exit door at the side of the building. A man was stumbling out of the bar, hands on his belt. He wore dark blue uniform pants and an untucked, stained wife-beater that was probably white once upon a time. A thick patch of curly black chest hair peeked out over the top of the shirt. He turned his back to the parking lot and leaned on the building with one hand while attempting to unzip his fly with the other, keeping his head down to avoid getting rain in his eyes.

"Jackpot."

Tommy mumbled under his breath.

"What?"

"Nothing, let's just get this over with."

They pulled their hoods up to cover their heads and jumped out of the van. Another benefit to the rain, it gave you an excuse to cover yourself. In less than ten strides, they were on the drunk man, one standing on each side of him. James waited for the man to finish urinating, shake himself off, and zip back up before he slapped him on the back of his wet shirt.

"Hey man, how's it going?"

"Heeeeyyyyy," the drunk said as he turned around, his grin showing off a couple of holes where teeth should have been. Heavy eyelids covered most of his dark brown eyes, and his skin was weather-worn and rough.

"Howsitgoinn?"

"Aw, we're all right, ain't we?" James nodded in Tommy's direction.

"Yep," mumbled Tommy.

"We're just gonna help you get to your car is all, looks like you could use a hand." James put one arm around the drunk's waist and started to walk to the back of the bar, towards the beach.

"That's nice..." the man said, his eyes half closed. When he realized where they were going, he pulled away from James and Tommy. "Eeeehhhh, my car's the other way!"

"Yeah, we're going for a swim first, you like to swim?" James pulled him back onto the foot path that led through the dunes.

The man mumbled to himself as the three of them shuffled down towards the water. Several times he had to lean on James or Tommy as his unsteady feet navigated the sandy path. James stopped them all once they were at the edge of the surf. "Now," he said with a flourish, waving his arm, "is the main event."

He shoved the man in the back with a grunt, sending the drunk face down into the sand. A second after he was down, his arms reached out in an alcohol-delayed reaction.

"Okay, Tommy, can you not be a *total* waste of flesh and give me a hand this time?"

Tommy glanced behind them, making sure they weren't followed, before he leaned down to sit on the man's back. It didn't take an extraordinary amount of strength to keep the man down on the sand, as he was already three beer-soaked sheets to the wind. James squatted next to them and wriggled a frayed wallet out of the man's back pocket.

"Let's see what we got here," he peeked into the folds of the wallet and whistled while he pulled out a wad of twenties.

"Nice, man I love payday, don't you?"

Tommy, still leaning on the man's back, looked up at James and rolled his eyes. "Yeah, it's great. *Love* it. Done?"

"Yeah, well, almost." James pulled the rich fisherman's knife out of his pocket, its ivory handle glinting in the rain.

"Hey, you don't have to… he's not gonna remember us, look at him!" Tommy gestured towards the man who had stopped wriggling and remained laying on the sand with his eyes closed, snoring. He was in that deep sleep only drunks can attend to.

"I know I don't *have* to." James balanced on his heels, careful not get sand on his jeans.

"You know, we could just leave him here. Let the tide come in and take care of everything for us," Tommy pleaded.

"But that's no fun." James touched the tip of the knife to the man's ear and traced a path down his jaw, the skin dented in but stopped just short of tearing.

"Well I don't have to watch, screw this." Tommy pulled his hood further over his face and walked back towards the dunes.

James pressed the knife in harder as he traced the shape of the drunk's jawline back up to his ear. Tiny beads of blood popped up in the blade's wake. Towards the bar, a cat screeched, and a bottle broke on the hard ground. He could barely see Tommy's outline in the parking lot lights as he headed towards their van.

James grabbed the man's thick brown hair and pulled back, lifting his chin towards the moonlight. He laid the serrated edge of the knife against his throat and leaned the tip into the soft flesh. In one motion, he shoved the point deep into the man's neck and pulled hard to the right. The drunk gasped, fully awake as blood pooled around his neck, making tiny rivers in the sand around him. James looked into his frightened eyes as the life slowly faded from them. It was a little different from the fisherman, but his heart still raced and there was a tightness in his jeans that hadn't been there before.

James took off at a brisk walk back through the dunes and into the parking lot of Hurricane's where Tommy was waiting.

"What did you do?" He shook his head, "Nevermind, I don't wanna know."

They slipped around the side of the building, taking a moment to verify the parking lot was clear, before stepping out. James whistled as they walked back to the van, ignoring Tommy's scowl.

Once they were inside and safely back on the road, Tommy turned to James. "James, look. I can't do this with you anymore. It just ain't right."

James glanced sideways at Tommy while he drove, one eyebrow raised.

Tommy continued, "This is serious shit! This ain't just robbin' people."

"You want out?"

"Well, yeah. I guess. I mean..." Tommy trailed off and looked down at his knees. He kept his eyes down as he brushed sand off his jeans.

James let the silence simmer as he pulled up to the traffic light and slowed to a stop. He took a deep breath and leaned towards Tommy, his mouth set in a hard line. "Look you little chicken shit. You need to unfuck yourself, and you need to do it quick. We got a good thing here and you're not gonna ruin it. Okay?"

Tommy grimaced and turned to look out the window. "Okay."

The light turned green and James pulled away, not believing for a minute that Tommy was going to be able to keep his cool.

22

⸻

"We really gotta get a new TV, I can't see shit around this crack." James settled further down into the white wicker chair, wincing as a loose piece of it scratched his leg. "And new chairs. This fucker's uncomfortable."

Sitting in the only other chair in the living room, another wicker masterpiece, Tommy's eyes were glued to his cell phone.

James leaned forward, "Hello, am I talking to myself?"

"What, you want new shit?" Tommy paused the video he was watching and glared at James. "With what money?"

"We'll make it happen, I'm tired of this trash."

"Whatever." Tommy went back to his phone.

James watched him, wondering when exactly he decided to start being a little bitch. Tommy used to be on board with whatever James wanted to do, no questions asked. But not lately. Ever since they killed that first guy and his kid ended up dying, Tommy hadn't been the same. He never had a problem being James' wing man before. When James broke into cars to grab purses or CD's or whatever, Tommy was his best lookout. When he slipped a few items in his pockets at the Grab 'n' Go, Tommy covered him. Hell, even when he cleaned out the register at the garage, Tommy was his alibi. Trey still had his suspicions and fired James anyway, but Tommy had his back. Always. But maybe that was his line in the sand, killing people.

It's not like they were innocent or anything. That drunk at the bar shouldn't have been so fucking plastered, James probably saved someone's life. If he had gotten in his car and driven home, he could have caused a wreck or some shit. The rich fisherman douche was a joke, trying to be like a good 'ole boy and fish for the day. He was using the wrong lures and couldn't cast for shit. Guy was an idiot. And Martin, well Martin was just an asshole. He was doing everyone a favor, taking care of those guys.

Tommy needed to get on board, and quick. James couldn't have him thinking about what was right or what was wrong, or who to tell his secrets to. As far as he knew, he was Tommy's only friend, so he didn't have to worry about him spilling his guts over a beer when he was the only one Tommy ever drank with. He was more worried about that detective.

"Hey Tommy."

"What?" he mumbled, still focused on his phone.

"You know that detective that came over the other day? Burns or Barnes or some shit?"

Tommy's mouth tightened, but his eyes stayed on his phone. "Yeah."

"Has he tried to talk to you, like, has he called you or anything? I mean, you'd tell me, right?" James leaned towards Tommy, putting his elbow on the arm rest and his chin in his hand.

Tommy looked up from his phone, staring into James' eyes without blinking. "Of course. And no, I haven't talked to him. Why?"

"Well…"

A bright flash of light caught James' eye, drawing his attention back to the TV. The screen was filled with an orange and red blaze. As the cameraman zoomed out, you could see the Lucky S store off to the left. On the right, something was definitely on fire. Looked like a van. A ratty one from the looks of it, but it was hard to tell since it was on fire. And wet. Water poured out in steady streams from the fire engines, filling the parking lot and overflowing onto the street in front of it. The evening's rains had stopped, unfortunately, leaving a thick blanket of warm moisture hanging just above everything. Lights from the police cruisers, the fire engines, and the reporters' cameras competed on every glistening surface, casting reflections of red, yellow, and blue into the night.

"Damn, check that out."

The video cut off abruptly, and Amy Andrews came back into view standing in front of a charred van. She was a tight piece of ass, but she looked like the kind of bitch who knew she was hot. All the hot ones did. They'd prance around in their little dresses or tight shirts, rubbing up on you in the club but getting all pissy if you touched their ass. Bitch or not, James was getting a semi just watching her. They knew what they were doing, putting her on TV in that tight ass blue dress. They knew all the hot-blooded young men would be tuned in, tongues wagging, not really listening to what she had to say but tuned in anyway.

"The victim was forty-four-year old Arthur Washington, a resident of League City..." Amy purred to the viewers.

"Hey look Tommy, it's that detective." James pointed at the TV.

Barnes was front and center, chest puffed out like Amy had chosen him specifically.

"Detective Barnes, is this connected to the Intracoastal Canal Killings?"

"The what?" His chest fell and his smile faded as he looked at her, confused.

"The Intracoastal Canal Killings, I believe the victims are Jon and Oliver Crow, and Leon Phillips?"

"Wait now, this probably has nothing to do with that. Oliver Crow's death hasn't been ruled a homicide yet, and

Jon Crow is still missing. I can't comment anymore on that, you know this is an ongoing investigation."

"But what about Leon Phillips? Does his murder have anything to do with the Crow incident? His body was found on the other side of the Canal, close to where the Crows' car was pulled out of the water."

All previous excitement at standing next to Amy faded. Apparently Amy's long legs were only going to get her so far in that interview. Detective Barnes was done. "We have no further comment at this time," he said with a frown before he walked off camera.

James chuckled to himself. "Exit blue-balled detective."

Amy turned to face the viewers, not missing a beat. "Leon Phillips was shot to death, not far from where Oliver Crow drowned. Now another body has shown up, also driving an older model van. Is this a coincidence? Or are we looking at the beginnings of a serial killer? Stay tuned to WBJ 39 for an exclusive interview with Arthur Washington's widow, tonight at five."

Tommy's gaze was frozen on the cracked television. His eyes wide, he slowly turned to look at James. "What the hell? Did you do that?"

"What? Hell no! I don't know anything about the van guys. I swear."

Tommy's eyes narrowed, and he shifted in his chair, James could tell he didn't believe him, but he also didn't give a shit what Tommy thought. Instead, another idea was beginning to form. "Hey Tommy, both of those guys drove old vans. I drive an old van. Think there's something to that?"

He hesitated before answering, still not convinced that James was innocent. "I don't know, but it *is* weird."

"Yeah."

Tommy jumped up and grabbed his keys off the hook by the front door. "I'm gonna be late for work, Mikel's later?"

"Yeah, I'll be there. I'm gonna stop by Uncle Bennie's first, see if he needs any help." Uncle Bennie owned a plumbing company and every now and then let James tag along for a few extra bucks.

After Tommy left, James sat in the uncomfortable chair still thinking about the vans. It was probably nothing, but he had learned that coincidences were few and to pay attention to the little things. Still, it was a stretch. He shrugged it off and went into the kitchen. He was probably being paranoid; he'd been around Tommy too damn much lately.

23

Rebecca leaned against the edge of the sink in the kitchen and listened to the coffee maker putter as it dripped water through the grounds and into the pot below. Above the dirty dishes was a window to the back yard, framing a large oak tree that oversaw the small fenced in space. Gray moss fluttered as it floated from the branches. Underneath the hanging moss was a well-used swing set. The chains creaked as the swing slowly rocked; an invisible wind pushing an invisible child. Attached was a slide with water pooled at the bottom from last night's storm, and a few branches from the tree had fallen around it. Rebecca grabbed a dishtowel and was halfway to the back door before realizing she didn't need to wipe down the slide. There was no longer a soggy-bottomed boy to worry about.

The shrill ringing of her cell phone filled the quiet kitchen.

It was her dad, and Rebecca ended the call more exhausted than when she had begun. She didn't understand why he actually wanted to be a dad just then. But, they *were* both alone. Wife number three had left him and was in the process of trying to take half of his retirement, all of his furniture, and most of his pride with her. Assets not-withstanding, it was for the best, but it still hurt. No matter what the reasons, divorce still hurt. It was a pain in the ass to divide things, and to bury a future you didn't even know was sick.

Wife number three had been sleeping with their realtor, Jeff Keys. Her dad said he was pretty sure that wasn't in the contract, but then muttered that he never read those things anyway. Rebecca wasn't surprised; it was only a matter of time before that marriage imploded. The woman was practically Rebecca's age, and had nothing in common with her dad. Well, that wasn't true, they both loved his money. Not that he had a lot of it, they weren't rich by any means. But, from what Rebecca had seen, the woman had taken a pretty significant step up on the social ladder when she married her dad. She got stability and a shopping allowance, and he got a beautiful woman by his side. Rebecca supposed they both knew exactly what their marriage was from the beginning, but the way her dad was mourning its demise, maybe not. He seemed to be genuinely heartbroken. He thought they were planning a future, buying a new home together. He had even talked about having more kids. But while he was dreaming, she was hiding money away in another bank account and screwing the realtor in every house he showed her.

He said he wanted to come visit, to make sure she was doing okay. Rebecca supposed that was normal, for a dad to show concern for a daughter, but it wasn't in their relationship to care beyond the surface. She had never lamented that fact; it was just how they were. How they had always been, even before her mom died.

Rebecca was still in high school when her mother's doctors found lung cancer. Her death a year later was a relief for everyone, she was in so much pain towards the end. The amount of medicine and pain killers she needed to survive left her in a near catatonic state. She stopped being Rebecca's mother long before she actually gave in to the cancer that had ravaged her body. Rebecca graduated high school three months after they put her mom in the ground, left for University, and hadn't looked back. Sometimes she regretted that move and thought she should have stayed for her dad. She had lost a mother but he had lost his wife, his life partner. But those three months she *was* there, he only went through the motions, a shadow of the man he used to be. He went to work and came home, ate dinner and watched TV. When Rebecca would come down for school in the morning, he'd have already left for work. When she got home late after her shift at the movie theater, he would be asleep in his chair in the living room.

She didn't send out graduation invitations, or take senior pictures. She did splurge on a class ring. It was a small dainty thing, though, not the big bulky traditional kind, and she'd paid for it with her own money. She tried hard not to ask him for anything; she knew he had been through enough already and she didn't want to add to his stress. When she saw him at graduation, sitting alone in the stands surrounded by grinning families, Rebecca was reminded of what could have been. Happy moms and dads, some with other kids, some with other adults, all proud to see their kid graduate. Her dad didn't look proud, sitting there alone. He looked sad.

But still, now he sounded like he wanted to come see her. He said he thought she was lonely and could use some company. She *was* lonely, but he couldn't take Oliver's place, or Jon's. She was able to put him off, but she knew she wouldn't be able to forever. He would come see her, and at least it would finally stop him from calling, checking off some obligatory box in his head of how he should behave after his daughter lost her family. He would then go back to his home in San Antonio and they would call each other on Christmas, birthdays, Father's Day, and that would be it. Back to their status quo.

With her phone still in her hand, she dialed Detective Barnes. He didn't answer, as usual. Rebecca supposed he was pretty busy; there *had* been a lot of murders in the area lately, so she left him the standard message to call her back. She no longer cried or pleaded with him to find her husband. She didn't have anything left in her anymore. She *was* curious about what they knew about the two murders. Did they know it was her? She didn't think so, or surely Barnes would be answering his phone. Rebecca only hoped that they would find something in the old man's van that belonged to Jon or Oliver, something that would close the case for them... for her. Of course, she didn't ask that, but she was hoping he would have news for her when he did call back.

Her stomach grumbled, reminding her that she hadn't eaten all day. A quick look in the fridge revealed a very old, moldy casserole she couldn't identify, a half bottle of ketchup, and an expired jug of milk. She grabbed her things and headed for the front door, it would do her good to get out of the house anyway.

The sun beat down through a cloudless sky as Rebecca drove away from her house. After the previous storm, the air hung thick and steamy around her, and water pooled in ditches and potholes. She drove with the windows down, soaking in the warmth from the sun. She headed down Plum Street and took a left onto Miller, away from the busy shopping center. Instead, she headed towards the meat market over on Kiber. There was a small taqueria in the back, where she liked to have barbacoa tacos, a Mexican coke, and a quiet corner to sit in.

There, no one knew she had buried a child, and no one would hug her or want to *talk* about it or give her *the look*. It had always been her favorite place to be alone. Funny, with a toddler, a husband, and work, she used to relish her alone time. She had worked hard to seek out quiet moments, and they came all too rarely. Most days she hid in the bathroom for a bit of peace. Her husband joked that she had intestinal issues, but she was pretty sure he knew what she was doing in there. Which was absolutely nothing. She wasn't arguing with a toddler, or making snacks, or any other tiresome mommy activity. Unfortunately, now, that's all she had. Quiet moments. Quiet days, with fleeting moments of noise and human interaction; moments with the TV on, when the detective called, or when Beth from work stopped by with another casserole. Then it was quiet again.

La Michoacana Meat Market sat between an oil change shop and an abandoned building. There were vague memories of a Chinese buffet restaurant being in that space before, but she wasn't positive. That end of town hadn't thrived since they built the new highway, and cars no longer needed to drive by to get to where they were going. Apparently they had just enough business to stay open. Covering the front door were fliers for Tejano and Mariachi bands, benefit dinners for lost loved ones, and ads for everything from babysitting to lawn mowing. Rebecca wondered why anyone would allow a stranger to babysit their child.

As she opened the door, mouth-watering aromas awakened her taste buds, and a juke box in the corner belted a Spanish song too loud for anyone to enjoy. To her left, an older Mexican woman sat at a small table with a pile of receipts and an adding machine. Her long gray hair was piled in a loose bun, and a cup of coffee sat in front of her. Next to her, a slender young woman folded silverware into paper napkins and stacked them in a gray dish bin. The old woman looked up as Rebecca passed, and smiled and nodded her chin in a greeting before she returned to her receipts. They knew Rebecca by sight, if not by name. She returned the nod as she walked by and headed towards the back of the building.

Past the butcher counter was a small room consisting of three booths covered in torn maroon plastic upholstery. A sturdy old cash register sat on a chipped counter, flanked by a basket of milk candy and a plastic tub of chiclets. To the right of the counter, a window was cut into the wall between it and the kitchen. Rebecca slid into a booth in the corner, shifting past the slump in the cushion where the stuffing had flattened over the years. A waitress appeared with a red plastic basket of chips, two different kinds of salsa, and a laminated menu.

Before she could get to the bottom of the salsa bowls, the waitress placed her usual meal in front of her. There were five small corn tortillas filled with beef, cilantro, and onions, circling a small stack of radish slices and grilled peppers. The food was as good as it always was, no more and no less. The consistency was comforting. No matter what happened elsewhere, inside the walls of the Taqueria, you could count on good food and a seat where no one would bug you.

She lingered in the booth long after she stopped eating, her fingertips playing at the edges of the bandage on her left arm. Under the bandage, the remains of a painful burn reminded her of what she had done. She had made it right, had evened those unseen balances that hang above it all, but it still didn't *feel* right. She was still alone. Not quite a widow, since they hadn't found Jon's body, but she knew in her heart that he was no longer alive. He would have come home to her if he was. And there wasn't a word for a mother without a child. Heartbroken, despondent, angry... she could think of a plethora of words but none that identified what she had lost. She stacked her dishes, wiped down the table, and slid out of the booth, leaving over half the meal on her plate.

Rebecca didn't notice the man's watch until he was standing at the register in front of her, paying for his meal. It was rose gold with a black leather strap, ordinary at first, a watch you could see anywhere. But what caused her heart to stop was the green ring inside the face. Rebecca pretended to look at the dish of milk candy on the counter next to the man, so she could get a closer look. It was a Bulova. The Accutron II Alpha, to be exact. Rebecca wasn't a connoisseur of watches by any stretch of the imagination, but she knew that watch. That was Jon's watch. She had bought it for their one-year anniversary, back when they were still intoxicated with each other and filled with dreams. She had 'Until we're 70' inscribed on the bottom, an inside joke from a song they both loved. She eased closer to the man, breathing in a mixture of sweat and moldy water. She had a fish tank that smelled like that once, when she was small.

Sweat shone on his pale skin. He was tall, at least 6 foot 4, and broad shouldered. The top to his blue coveralls hung at his waist, revealing a stained white undershirt. He was bald, but his goatee and mustache were orange-blond. When he glanced over at Rebecca, his dark blue eyes shifted down her body, resting back on her face. There was no mistaking the hunger in them as he opened his mouth to speak. She moved back in disgust. He shrugged, continued paying, and turned to walk to the front of the market.

Rebecca threw down a ten, told the woman to keep the change, and hurried after the man. As she left the building she caught sight of him across the parking lot, opening the front door of a white van. Emblazoned along the side in green were the word 'EZ Plumbing'. Next to it, a smiling cartoon man held a plunger while water droplets rained down around him.

Rebecca rushed to her car and put it into drive. Confused, she wasn't sure what she was doing, only that she needed to follow that man. It had to be him, he had Jon's watch on. It couldn't be a coincidence, him having Jon's watch *and* getting into an old van. It had to be him, there was no other explanation for it. He was the man who had killed

Ollie.

All thoughts of the man she had burned in the 'Lucky S' parking lot vanished as she leaned on the gas pedal and hurried after the plumber's van. They took a left out of the parking lot onto Plum Street and blended with the traffic heading North.

"We got him, Ollie."

From the backseat, Oliver caught his Mother's eye in the rear-view mirror and smiled. Pale round cheeks squished up towards his eyes and a giggle floated across the car and into the front seat where Rebecca sat, determined and more than a bit unhinged.

24

"Hey, are you still in town? Looks like the AAA guy is here already, we'll just ride with him. You can meet us at the mechanic shop, it's closer to home anyway."

"I'm not, but I can turn around. They got there fast."

"Yeah, I thought so too. But he's not in a tow truck. This is probably the car service so we don't have to ride with the tow guy. Either way, they really need to invest in nicer vehicles. This van looks like it's about to fall apart. I'll call you back when we're on the road again. Love you."

Jon opened the driver's side door and flipped the trunk latch, "Hey buddy, you doing okay?"

Nothing.

He leaned across the seat to peer into the back seat, where Oliver had been singing and talking just a few minutes before. He was still there, eyes closed tightly, and head tilted to the side. Jon chuckled. The beach did it for him, every time. The combination of scorching sun, running around in the hot sand, and swimming against the currents, had always been a fast ticket to a long nap.

Jon left the car in neutral and closed the door with a soft click. Just ahead, the van had navigated the rocky side road and was creeping along towards him. But unless they had started offering plumbing services along with roadside assistance, it wasn't AAA. The words 'EZ Plumbing' screamed at him garishly from the side of the van in bright green paint. He would have bet money it glowed in the dark. Beside the text, an obnoxious cartoon plumber danced in the rain with his fist wrapped around a plunger. Jon's shoulders sagged as he rummaged in the trunk. Perhaps the spare tire would materialize if he stared hard enough at the empty space where it should have been.

In the van, a bald white man was dancing his fingers on the steering wheel along with the radio, every beat a tap-tap on the faded black plastic. He was technically on the clock, hence the van, but his boss didn't care about what he didn't know. The last job had only taken a minute, so it wasn't like he was running behind or anything. The gray haired old Mexican lady in the bright blue house on stilts over on Crab St. had lost her wedding ring down the sink. Five minutes in the P-trap, and he had produced a soap-scum covered ring. The woman had practically cried and began telling him all about her dead husband in stilted English. He got out of there as fast as he could.

That's when he saw the blue Chevy down by the water, just as he was about to pull onto the bridge. Glancing at the clock on the dashboard, he figured he'd go see what was up. Looked like an easy enough take, anyway. The car didn't look like much, but you never knew what kind of money people were carrying around with them. As he pulled closer, he could tell it was a flat tire by the way the car sat tilted up on one end. A man had already jacked it up to get it ready for the new tire and was standing in front of the trunk with his back to the van, looking down. Yeah, it was going to be an easy take.

A bright flash of light flickered through the passenger side window. Under the bridge, a shiny silver bike leaned against its rusted kick stand. The evening sun shone directly on it, throwing reflections around the dark underside of the bridge like confetti. Another bike, not as shiny, had been dropped into the dust, and a few more lay hidden in the shadows of the bridge. Standing nearby was a small group of kids. Well, probably older teenagers but everyone under the

178

age of twenty seemed like a kid to him. One of them sort of looked like his nephew, but he couldn't get a good look. That boy didn't know how to stay out of trouble. Tall, pale as a ghost, gangly, and a head full of wayward red curls, the boy was leaning against a large rock, smoking something. He'd bet money on it being a doobie and not a cigarette. The man leaned over the passenger seat to get a better look...

He must have been closer to the parked car than he realized, and he swore he only took his eyes off it for a second, but a second was all it took. In the time he had spent analyzing the kid under the bridge, his van had continued traveling towards the parked blue Chevy. A thud, a jolt, and a muffled scream brought his attentions back to the front of his van. Directly in front of him was the blue car. Technically it was slightly under his front bumper, but no one was arguing with him. The only other person around was caught between the two vehicles, legs pinned and eyes wide, staring straight at him through the grimy windshield of the van.

The guy must have been in shock. Anyone would have been, with their bottom half squished all up like that and their top half just frozen there. His mouth gaped open, gasping and trying to take in air. His chest, caught between the hood of the van and the back frame of his car, was sunken inwards in a most unnatural way.

The 'good Samaritan' slammed his van into park, threw his door open, and hurried to the man's side. There was a lot of blood coming from high up on his legs, spurting and spattering onto the vehicles and into the dirt below. The man grunted repeatedly, each sound smaller than the previous, until there were no more sounds, and he lay slumped forward onto the hood of the van. The driver stood watching in morbid fascination, just out of reach of the pool of blood in the dust. Sure, he had seen people die before, but never like that. Dirt and gravel crunched beneath the Chevy's

179

tires as it inched towards the water, set in motion by the impact while the man, no longer pinned upright, slumped to the ground in a cloud of dust.

The plumber glanced furtively towards the bridge and the darkness beneath, but the kids were gone, leaving nothing but shadows and ashes in their wake. It probably wasn't his nephew, anyway. He bet they all had high-tailed it out of there the minute his van hit that man. They had the right idea, that's what he needed to do, get out of there. It looked like the issue was going to take care of itself anyway, the car was still on a steady roll towards the water's edge. With any luck, it would go in and he wouldn't need to deal with it drawing attention. By the time anyone else decided to pull off the road for a quick wiz or a make out session, he'd be long gone and headed to another plumbing emergency.

Halfway back to his van he had an idea and jogged back to the man on the ground. There was his back pocket, staring straight up at the sky, with the tell-tale square indention puffed out. The driver leaned down, wriggled the man's wallet out of his pocket, grabbed his watch for good measure, and scurried back to his van. No sense letting a good opportunity go to waste.

25

Rebecca followed the white van down Plum Street, past struggling mom and pop businesses and run-down homes. The eclectic mixture of residential and commercial lots left a palpable identity crisis. An old concrete building marked 'Discount Dental' kept company with a 'Tom's Pawn', a home topped with mismatched roofing shingles, and a 'La Vida Regional' church. The van slowed as it approached a square house on the left with tan walls and black trim, before pulling into its gravel driveway. The house had seen better days and sagged on its wooden foundation. She thought it was fitting, a man like that didn't deserve to have nice things, and he didn't deserve to live.

Half a block down from the tan house, she eased onto the side of the road and killed the engine. Rebecca hunched low in the seat and held her breath while the man walked up a few steps to a small porch on the side of the house. He checked a mail-box hanging to the left of the door, pulled out a handful of papers, and walked inside.

With no other cars in the guy's driveway, it looked like no one else was home, at least not anyone with car. Rebecca wiped the sweat off her forehead and onto her shorts. The car was getting damn hot, but she couldn't risk turning the engine back on, so she cranked her window down to let in some fresh air. Though really, fresh air was no part of the Texas summer, it was still better than baking in the car. In her rear-view mirror, once again, Oliver sat in his booster in the middle of the back seat. He giggled and sang to himself while Rebecca forced her eyes forward, afraid he would disappear again if she turned around. She sat in the oppressive heat swatting mosquitoes for twenty minutes before summoning the courage to get out of her car.

Resisting the urge to look in the backseat, she whispered, "I'll be back, Ollie. I'm going to make this right."

Pulling the gun from her glove box, she was still surprised by the weight of it. She figured she would never get used to it, but after that day it wouldn't matter. Rebecca's mission was to make it right, the horrible thing that man had done. Then, she would return home and put the gun in her nightstand like every other American, never to look at it again. The gun, and that man, would never be thought of again after that day. She placed it in the front pocket of her jeans and untucked her T-shirt. With the bulge sticking out against her slim frame, she knew it wasn't well hidden, but unless she wanted to wear a sweltering jacket, it was her only option.

She looked up and down the street before getting out of her car. Thankfully, the street was empty. So close to the end, the last thing she needed was a witness. Everyone was either getting their teeth pulled, counting their offering money, or inside their homes napping on the hot July afternoon. A small dog, half beagle and half rat, jogged by, turning its head briefly to bark in confusion at her presence before continuing down the road.

"Yeah, I know. I won't be here long," she muttered.

Traffic roared in the distance and a couple of birds sang to one another as she sidestepped puddles in the road on her way to the small house. It wasn't long before she was standing on his porch. Peeling green paint on the front door revealed shades of dirty white underneath, and the window screens to her left were ripped and worn. Rebecca reached into her pocket and gripped the gun with her right hand, using the knuckles of her left to rap on the door.

A deep voice echoed from the back of the house, "Coming!"

When he opened the door, an Astros T-shirt and black basketball shorts had replaced the blue coveralls. His hair dripped water onto his shoulders, and he held a damp towel in his hand. A minty soap smell wafted out onto the front porch, a marked improvement from his earlier stench.

"Can I help you?" he asked.

"It was you," she replied. Her hand dripping perspiration as it gripped the gun in her pocket.

"I'm sorry? What was me?"

"You killed him, and you left my baby there." Her voice raised to a near yell. "You left him!"

He shook his head and muttered as he closed the door, "Crazy bitch."

Tears streamed down her face as she pulled the gun out of her pocket, her hand still clenched around the handle. She turned the doorknob, surprised to see it open. He really was an arrogant piece of work, assuming she wouldn't want to come in after him and try to make it right. He probably didn't even realize what he had done or had already forgotten. Men like him only cared about themselves. When she barged into the room, he stopped halfway down the hallway and turned to face her, disbelief blanketing his face. Without hesitation, Rebecca fired a shot at his chest, the biggest part of him she'd have the most luck hitting. She kept firing; at his head, his legs, his stomach, back to his chest, until the gun was almost empty, and he had slumped to the floor. He reached out with his hands and pulled himself an inch at a time towards a door at the end of the hallway. Probably a bedroom where, she guessed, he also had a dusty gun in his nightstand.

Rebecca closed the door behind her and turned the lock. The man had made it halfway down the short hallway, not looking back as he put all his energy into getting to that door. He never saw her as she knelt down and touched the gun to the bare skin at the back of his head. He stiffened at the cold touch of metal, but before he could react, she fired again, her last bullet. Smoke curled from the back of his head, away from the dark red blood spilling onto his pale scalp. His elbows slid out from underneath him and his raised shoulders fell to the floor. His head lay sideways at an awkward angle, forever staring at the chipped paint on the wall.

She leaned over him, breathing in the mixture of minty soap and coppery blood. The gun was empty, but still sat heavy in her hand, weighing on her to do *more*. Rebecca lifted the gun as high as she could reach, and brought it down hard against the back of the man's bare skull. Blood from the bullet hole spurted up around her, coating her and the wall that his lifeless eyes stared at, as she brought it down again and again. She didn't remember stopping, only that she found herself in the kitchen, washing blood off her hands and arms, and looking around for something to wrap the gun in. It was covered in dark red grime, pulpy bits of flesh, and gray brain tissue. Behind her, what was left of the man who had killed her son lay in pieces on the hardwood floor.

A sharp rap on the door pulled her attention away from the dead bastard splayed out in the hallway. She tip-toed to the side of the living room window and peered through the blinds. An old woman with curlers knotted around thin gray hair stood there, wide eyes darting back and forth. Rebecca jerked away from the window before she could be seen.

"Tulley! I told you to keep that damn music down!" She adjusted the top of her floral muumuu, causing her large breasts to send pink and blue wildflowers swaying back and forth. "God damn noisy kids, can't an old woman have any peace?" She rapped on the door again, louder this time. "I know you're in there! I see your van!" The woman wasn't going anywhere soon, she looked like she had all the time in the world to stand there in her gown and flip-flops.

Rebecca stepped back from the front of the house and walked towards the kitchen. Her soft-soled slip-on shoes whispered against the wooden floor. To the left of a sink piled with dirty dishes was a door that led to the backyard. With a quick glance back, she slipped through the door and into the back yard. In front of her was a small space covered primarily in dirt. A broken fence marked its three sides, and neglected flower beds sat to the right. She realized she could hear a dog barking from the street, probably that same rat-looking one from earlier. The old woman had stopped yelling at the front door. Rebecca risked a glance around the side of the house and saw her shuffling down the street, holding her muumuu tight around her.

The broken fence was just loose enough for her to slip through and into a small alley that ran behind the back yards of houses on either side. She saw the small, ugly dog from earlier having a heated discussion with a large mutt. Lucky for the little dog, there was a pretty strong chain link fence between them. Little guys always seemed to have more balls when there wasn't a chance in hell they'd actually get into a fight. As she got closer, both dogs turned towards her and kept barking. She picked up her pace as she passed them, hurrying to the end of the alley.

***

Once home, Rebecca stripped in the garage and walked naked through the side kitchen door towards the bathroom. A long hot shower took care of most of her issues; she'd deal with the clothes the next day. She plopped onto the couch with a glass of wine in one hand and the remote control in the other, a warm fluffy robe tied snugly around her waist.

For the next few hours she scanned channels without hearing what any of them had to say. She should have been relieved, but she wasn't. All she could think about was all that blood, and whether or not she left any fingerprints anywhere, and if someone saw her... but once the wine had a chance to spread over her like a heavy blanket, she dropped the remote onto the coffee table and finally closed her eyes.

26

James leaned forward, resting his elbows on the time-worn wooden bar in front of him. "Fucking new stools, whose idea was this?" he muttered to himself. The old chairs *were* pretty beat up, but at least they had a back support. Abe had been making so many changes lately, pretty soon Mikel's Pub wouldn't even be recognizable. All in the name of 'progress' and 'appealing to the younger crowd'. James thought there was absolutely nothing wrong with the bar staying exactly the way it was, at least the way it had been for the last five years he and Tommy had been going there. They first came in for the cold beer but stayed for the killer burgers. You had to get there early, before the kitchen shut down for the night; after that they would only sell you mini bags of chips, peanuts, and microwave pizzas. It wasn't too bad, even if you did miss the kitchen. Mikel's was small for a bar, but cozy, and you knew most everyone who walked through the door. There was one pool table in the back, and an electronic dart game on the wall. It definitely looked better later in the day, when sunlight wasn't streaming through the front windows, piercing the haze of smoke and highlighting every scuff mark on the floor. French fries, burgers, and cigarettes all mingled in the air, smelling better than any woman he had ever known. To him, at least. He never had use for those expensive perfumes and shit.

He took a bite of his cheeseburger and sighed, closing his eyes. No one else made them like that. Not those fancy restaurants over on harbor-side, not even the food trucks down on the beach. He didn't know what their secret was, and he was okay with that. As long as they kept cranking them out exactly the way they were. They used a jalapeno sourdough bun, none of that sesame seed bullshit, and when you took a bite, grease oozed out of the meat and dripped down onto your plate. It was exactly like mama used to make. Well, someone else's mama.

That day, it was still early enough to catch the kitchen but late enough that a few of the night crowd had already trickled in. Old Man Dennis sat on his left, picking at his french fries. A greasy napkin on his plate was the only evidence that a burger had ever sat there. Two women were standing in front of the jukebox, flipping through the pages. They couldn't have been a day over eighteen, probably fresh from the nursing school down the street, looking to have some fun. James would bet money their ID's were as fake as their tans. Too young for him, anyway. Pretty to look at, and he'd bet fun to fuck, but they came with too much drama and immaturity. He turned back to his half-eaten burger and looked at his watch. Tommy would be there any minute but you never knew when he had to stay late to finish up a car. Trey could be a real hard ass sometimes.

He had just wiped the last of the grease from his chin when Tommy walked in, still wearing his blue coveralls. His shoulders were tight and he didn't look up at James as he jerked out the empty stool next to him and sat down.

"Hey Tommy, whatcha havin'?" Abe asked as he picked up Dennis' empty plate and wiped down the counter.

"Bacon burger, extra fries," Tommy answered.

Abe pointed to the clock on the wall. "Sorry, kitchen closed about ten minutes ago."

Tommy sighed and finally looked at James. "Really, you couldn't have ordered me something before they closed? You knew I was coming."

James shrugged and continued to eat his fries.

"You could have at least shared." Tommy glared at James before turning to the bartender. "I guess just give me a Bud and a bag of the sour cream chips."

A gust of warm air and harsh light from the street lamps swept across the bar as the front doors blew open. A large man stepped in, tall and broad-shouldered, his long black hair braided halfway down his back and a biker vest zipped snugly across his chest. Behind him was a smaller man, dirty blond hair cut short and wearing the same vest. Their eyes roamed the bar, slowly adjusting to the low light, before falling on James and Tommy.

They both smiled. "Sup James, Tommy. Ya'll wanna play a quick game? Andrew here got us kicked off league tonight so we ain't got nothin' else goin."

A local pool league often held tournaments over at Hurricane's Bar; no serious player usually wanted to slum it by hitting around on the ripped felt at Mikel's.

"Sure," said James.

"Not tonight," said Tommy

James looked at Tommy with eyebrows raised. "Come on, it's just one game. What else do we have to do? It's not like you gotta sit down to eat those chips." One corner of his mouth tipped up in a sarcastic smile.

Tommy took a deep breath before answering, "I'm tired. Tired and hungry. Some of us have been working all day."

"All right, see ya'll later." The two men picked up the tray of balls from Abe and headed to the back of the room.

Tommy chewed his chips quietly, staring at his beer.

"What crawled up your ass?" James asked.

"Nothin'."

"Like hell, nothing. You've been cranky as a bitch on the rag lately, and now you don't even wanna play pool?"

"I'm just tired of it, is all." Tommy laid a five on the bar and stood up. "I'm gonna go grab some food and head home."

"Hold on now." James jerked a ten-dollar bill out of his wallet, slapped it on the counter, and scrambled to catch Tommy at the door. "I'll walk out with you. Need to talk anyway."

They walked towards the alley in silence, Tommy with his hands shoved into his pockets and a scowl on his face. A few cars passed by on the main street, but none turned down the alley where they always parked. No one parked there unless they wanted their windows smashed in and their stereo stolen. James had one up on them though: he didn't have a stereo. He wasn't afraid of much anyway, including dark alleys and whoever might be lurking there. Shit, they should be scared of him, he thought as his fingers curled around the smooth pearl handle of the knife in his pocket.

"Well, bye," Tommy mumbled as he pulled his keys out of his pocket.

James glanced behind them before following Tommy into the shadows.

"Hey Tommy."

"What," he said, without turning around. A chirp emitted from his car as he unlocked the door.

"You've been a real pain in the ass lately, you know that?"

Tommy glanced back at James. "Whatever, man."

"I'm just saying, I don't know if this arrangement is gonna work out anymore."

"What are you talkin' about?" With one hand on his car door, he turned towards James. He barely saw the street light glinting off the sharp blade before it was buried to the hilt in his stomach. Tommy gasped, his eyes wide with shock. He pulled on James' hands still holding the blade and jerked backwards, freeing himself from the knife. He knew what James was capable of, so he had to know where he was headed. Tommy turned to run but James grabbed his arm and pulled him down onto the dirty concrete. He fell with a splash into a puddle of foul-smelling rainwater left over from the previous storm.

Tommy wrenched sideways into James' legs, just below the knee. James buckled and fell down next to him. James could feel his knees burn through his jeans as they scraped against the hard ground. He managed to get a punch across Tommy's jaw, but it wasn't enough to knock him out, since James was still unsteady and Tommy was fighting back harder than he'd ever seen him fight before. Looked like he wasn't such a little bitch after all, thought James. He'd still have to kill him, but he felt a little better about his friend not being such a pussy.

Tommy gripped James' knife-wielding hand and twisted, trying to get him to release the blade. James rolled over onto Tommy in an attempt to use his own body weight to pin him down. He had about fifty pounds on Tommy's small frame. Their breath came out in grunts and huffs, both getting tired, but James had the one-up. He was still the one with the knife. He wrestled his hand free from Tommy's grip and turned the blade back towards him.

For a split second, James looked into Tommy's eyes and saw the friend that had always been there for him. But it wasn't personal, it was necessary. He was the only other one that knew everything James had done and would do. Tommy was weak, and he was a liability.

James held Tommy's gaze as he pushed the blade into the soft flesh of his neck and jerked it to the side. Blood came out in spurts as Tommy gasped for breath, his hands trying to hold the cut together – like that was going to do any damn good. His head had fallen to his chin, the neck muscles no longer able to hold it up.

James pulled himself off the ground and brushed dirt

off his jeans as he watched the life flow out of Tommy, onto the gravel and concrete around him. His hands caught on the small tears of his jeans, right over his knees.

"Fuck." He could see bright red blood through the holes, some of it seeping through to the front of his jeans. He kicked Tommy's lifeless body. "These were new fucking pants, asshole."

Tommy stared at James, long after his pupils had dilated and his mouth had fallen open. It was no longer Tommy, of course. James figured he stopped being Tommy around the time they killed that guy and his kid. That's when he started acting more like a little bitch, anyway.

A strong stench of piss and shit wafted up from the ground, mingling with the already rancid odor of the alley. Disgusted, James turned towards his van. His key was in the door before he realized he needed to do something about the little scene he'd left behind. He looked towards the street before jogging back to Tommy's body. He knelt down and rolled Tommy over on his side just enough to pull his wallet out of his pants. As he got a good grip on the wallet, a groan slipped from Tommy's lips and James almost shit his pants. He yanked the wallet out and jumped back, expecting to hear Tommy start talking or crying, but nothing else came from his mouth.

Back in the van, he eased out of the alley, thankful that no one was around to finger him being there. He turned the radio to The Box and turned it up as high as he could stand it, bobbing his head along with the music. Traffic was light, and the moon was full. He was at their place in no time, wondering how long he'd be able to put off their landlord before he realized he wasn't getting any more rent checks. He just needed a couple more takes and he'd have enough to get out of town. Just a couple more.

After a shower and a change into clean clothes,

James had barely put his feet up on the coffee table when he heard footsteps on the stairs outside. He moved to the window and peeked out, wondering who the hell was coming by that late at night. His only friend was laying in an alley so he was pretty sure it wasn't him. Whoever it was, had parked where James couldn't see him. He closed the curtains just as a loud rapping came from the front door.

27

___

"James!" His mama rushed through the front door and smothered him in a tight embrace. "I'm so glad you're okay."

"Mama, what are you doing out so late?" he asked, his voice muffled in the folds of her arms. He tried to take a deep breath around the stench of grease, sweat, and dollar store body spray. "And why wouldn't I be okay?"

She finally released him and shuffled into the living room, the wicker chair creaking as she settled into it. Her face was flushed and her chest heaved up and down. "Ooh wee, those stairs nearly took me out this time! When you gonna move to somethin' without stairs?"

Her eyes darted around the small living room and back to James. "And where's Tommy?"

"I don't know. But mama, why wouldn't I be okay?" He crouched down in front of her chair and put his hand on her knee. Something was clearly worrying her, and he had no idea what it could be.

"I was watchin' the news and they said these guys was killed and did you know that *all* of them was drivin' vans that looked just like yours?" She paused to catch her breath. "I told Betsy, I said 'Betsy, now that's the kinda van James drives'. And she says, 'You better go tell him to sell it'. And you know, I think she's right. There's some crazy damn people in this world, James, and it's better to be safe than sorry, right?"

James chuckled and squeezed her knee, *"That's* what's got you so worked up? Shit, mama, I thought it was something serious!"

He straightened up and walked to the kitchen, talking

to her over his shoulder. "I'll get you a coke. Yeah, Tommy and I was watching that the other day, some dude burned up in a van, and one was shot next to another van. But ma, you know how many people drive vans? I mean, you got regular people, and then you got electricians, and plumbers, and all them. It's not that big of a coincidence that two people driving a van died. There's lots of vans." He pulled a can of cold Dr. Pepper out of the fridge.

"I'm not just talkin' 'bout the nigg…"

"Mama," James interrupted with a sigh, his eyes imploring her to do better. He popped the tab on the can and handed her the drink.

She took a big swig of Dr. Pepper and rolled her eyes, "Well whatever, I'm not just talkin' 'bout the *African American* man who caught on fire, and the guy under the bridge." She repositioned herself in the chair. "I'm talkin' about all them *and* that guy that was shot in his house the other day. Guess what was parked in his driveway?" She slapped her knee with her flat palm, "That's right, a goddamn van."

"Where was that?"

"Over off Plum, you know down by that wetback church."

"Mama, seriously."

"James Porter, I did not live no fifty-eight damn years just so my own child could tell me how to talk. You got more important things to figure out than how me, your grown ass *mama*, talks about – hey, what happened to your arm? You okay?"

He looked down at the scratches on his arm where the concrete and rocks from the alley had scraped a good two-inch gap open. The blood had long since dried and had come off in the shower. Only red angry skin around an ugly scab remained.

"Yeah, just fell down earlier, the sidewalk was all wet

from the rain. It's fine." He needed to change the subject. "What do you want me to do, mama, sell my van?"

She raised her voice, "If you have to sell it, James, then sell it. I'm not tryin' to be on TV cryin' over my dead son. Now you're all I got left in this world and I aim to make sure you're safe."

He walked back to the kitchen to grab himself a beer and froze holding the door of the fridge open, staring blankly inside. Dead son... dead son. He grabbed a Bud and slammed the door so hard the expired ketchup and mustard rattled on their shelf. Caught by a draft of air, a flutter of movement on top of the fridge caught his eye. He had almost forgotten about the pile of pictures and shit from that guy's wallet he had tossed up there weeks ago. That first guy he killed, under the bridge. He had a kid, a kid he and Tommy had sent off floating down the Intracoastal canal, and the kid had a mama who was on TV crying about her dead son.

"What you doin' in there?"

He set the beer on the counter and reached up to grab a handful of credit cards and pictures, sending a cloud of dust into the dark space above the fridge. "I'll be right there."

He sifted through them until he found the one he remembered. There, looking up at him, was the smoking hot wife, the fat ass soccer dad, and the dead kid posing in front of a Christmas tree. Their clothes all matched like the fucking uppity family they were. The man wore jeans with a red button-up shirt, the woman had on a white dress with a red belt, and the kid was wearing red suspenders over a white shirt. They were picture perfect. He looked closer at the wife, leaning in to try to see further into her big green eyes.

Maybe someone saw his van under the bridge, or maybe the husband said something to someone on the phone. James closed his eyes, trying to remember that night.

When he and Tommy first pulled up behind the blue Chevy, he couldn't recall if the man had a phone in his hand or not. He shook his head, he just didn't know. But even then, even if someone said or saw something, and it was known that a white van was involved, there's no way that woman was on some vigilante streak, she looked like a member of the goddamn PTA. There was just no way she was involved in anything like that. It was just a coincidence, the vans.

"James Porter, what in the hell is you doing in there?"

He stuck the picture in his back pocket and grabbed the Bud off the counter, "I'm coming."

It was a good hour before he was able to convince his mama that he wasn't going to be killed by some van-obsessed serial-killer. He closed the door behind her and pulled the picture from his pocket. Leaning against the back of the chair, he stared at the face of the woman. There was just no way that bitch could be out there killing people. It just seemed like a reach. He went back to the pile and fished out a driver's license. Jon Crow. He made note of the address and put everything but the picture back on the top of the fridge. If a detective *did* come knocking, he didn't want to make it easy on them and just have shit out for them to see. He was smarter than that.

***

James woke up at eight in the morning to Tommy's alarm clock blaring rock music through the thin wall that separated their bedrooms. Fucking Tommy and his goddamn alarm. He threw the covers off and walked, naked, over to Tommy's room. Another benefit of having a dead roomie, James could let it swing. He used to sleep naked all the time, but he didn't like how Tommy kept staring at his junk anytime he got up to use the bathroom, so he had taken to wearing boxers at night. He yanked the alarm clock's cord out of the socket it was plugged into and threw it against the wall before shuffling back to his own room.

No matter how long he laid in bed trying to go back to sleep, it just wasn't happening. Every time he closed his eyes, he saw that woman's face. It wasn't until he was up, showered, and eating leftover pizza, that he knew he needed to do something. He was still pretty sure she wasn't the one going around killing people, but curiosity was getting the better of him. He needed to know more about her. Besides having a dead husband and kid, of course.

He drove his van slowly down Palmer Street, taking in the manicured lawns and upper middle-class homes. He knew he'd never live in a neighborhood like that, no matter how many people he robbed. James was a realist, he didn't give a shit if his glass was half full or half empty, as long as it had a shot of whiskey in it. That was his philosophy. There wasn't nothing a shot of whiskey couldn't fix.

He glanced down at the driver's license in his hand again, checking the house number. That was it, 1418. He scanned the homes as he drove past, looking for the numbers. He wished they would all agree on one fucking place to put house numbers. There was 1412, then a house he couldn't tell, then he thought the next one should be 1416, but there was goddamn ivy growing on the front of the number plate. Which brought him to the next house, 1418. There was a black Ford Escort in the driveway, and what looked like an older model Mercury Cougar. The Cougar screamed police, from its long antennae stretching out of the top, to the searchlight mounted on the side.

Maybe the bitch *was* responsible for the killings, and she was finally getting what was coming to her. As he cruised past the house, he was able to glimpse inside the open curtains. There was the woman, it had to be her, sitting on a couch next to that nosy ass detective.

He stepped on the gas and took off before they could look up and see him. So maybe he wasn't going to go knock on her door, but at least he knew where she lived. He would be back, and he'd make damn sure no detective was there when he did.

28

"Hey baby," Rebecca's dad held his keys in one hand and a suitcase in the other. He was smiling, but his eyes betrayed the sadness within. "Is this a bad time?"

"No, I just... I'm surprised to see you is all." She led him into the house and locked the door behind him.

"Well I know you said you were fine, but I called your office yesterday and they said you were still out. So, I figured I needed to come down." He set his suitcase down in the front hall and dropped his keys on the small table against the wall. "Can I use your bathroom? It's been a long drive."

"Yeah of course, I'll put some coffee on."

"That sounds perfect," he said, as he limped down the hallway. His knees were getting worse and the drive hadn't helped them any. The doctor said he'd need a knee replacement in the next year, but he was fighting it pretty hard. Rebecca hadn't realized he was getting so bad. He wasn't limping like that when they were down for the funeral.

The coffee was already dripping when he returned, glistening hands held out in front of him, looking around for a hand towel. She pointed to a dry dish rag and poured them both a cup of coffee.

He closed his eyes and inhaled, "Aah, I've always loved that smell. Do you know they make a coffee scented candle now? Isn't that crazy? Paula bought me one for the study a few months ago." His voice caught on her name, still not used to the new way of thinking of her. "Eh, guess she wasn't all bad." He set the rag down on the counter.

Rebecca handed him his mug, "Dad, she banged your realtor, she was pretty much all bad."

The corners of his mouth turned up in a reluctant smile, "Yeah I guess you're right there."

She leaned against the counter and crossed her arms over her chest, "So, what's going on? What's the real reason you're here?"

He sighed and set his cup down, looking at her. "I had to get out of that house, it's so... empty – I mean... I'm sorry."

"It's okay, dad. My house is empty, your house is empty. We're all empty." Rebecca picked up her coffee cup, peered in it for a second, and twirled it to mix the contents.

"Yeah, but...I shouldn't complain. You've been through so much."

"It's okay, really. It gets my mind off things, you know?"

"Yeah I get that." He paused to take a long swig of his coffee before setting it back down and wiping his chin. "Well, I just couldn't be there anymore. She took almost all the furniture, except for that couch your mom and I had. She never liked it, said it looked like something her parents would own." He stopped to chuckle. "That's kind of ironic, now. I guess I was old enough to be her dad."

He cleared his throat and met her eyes. "So why aren't you back at work yet?"

"They told me to take more time, that it was too soon to be back. It's frustrating, really. Work is the one thing I *could* do right now." She knew the truth, that her co-workers weren't quite ready to be around her. The 'Hello's' and 'How are you's' would come with a tilt of the head and a pitiful look in their eyes, if they knew what happened. If it was someone who didn't know, would she return their cheerfulness like nothing was wrong to avoid any questions? Did she tell them, causing an awkward silence when they didn't know what to say back? It was all too exhausting, navigating a world where she was no longer Rebecca Crow: wife, mother, and accountant. The new Rebecca was a victim, someone to be held at a distance, because while they liked to think it couldn't possibly happen to them, they would still walk a wide circle around it. And her. People liked to go about their days in blissful ignorance of the violent world around them and when it edged in too close, they didn't know what to do but keep far away lest it be contagious.

"I get it bug, but don't wait too long, you know? You don't want to forget how to be a part of things."

He hadn't called her 'bug' since she was a child, she hated it then, but now... she didn't mind it so much. "I won't, I'll probably go back in a week or so. They can't make me take more time than I already have."

"What are you doing to stay busy? It's not good to be cooped up in the house all day."

"Not a whole lot." She glanced at his suitcase in the front hall. "How long are you staying?"

"Eh, just the weekend. Some of us *do* have to work, you know." He winked at her.

"They won't let me! I keep telling them I want to go back...*need* to go back." Rebecca's voice rose until she cut off with a huff. It wasn't a battle she was going to win, and her dad wasn't the problem, anyway. "Want a refill?"

"I'm good on coffee, but I am starving. I haven't eaten all day. Did you have lunch yet?"

At the mention of food, her stomach grumbled. She often forgot to eat, and her clothes showed it, hanging loosely on her already small frame. "Food sounds great. How about I call us in some Chinese?" She opened the junk drawer and leafed through it, looking for the take-out menu.

"Chinese is perfect. You call it in, I'll go pick it up. Do they have Orange Chicken?"

"They have everything. You still like extra egg rolls and that nasty mustard sauce?" She pulled the menu out of the drawer.

"Yep." He grinned.

He got up from the table and headed for the door, calling over his shoulder, "Want me to get us drinks also, or do you have stuff here?"

"Drinks would be…" A sharp rapping sounded from the front door.

Her dad was only a step away so he opened it, to a surprised Detective Barnes standing there with his knocking fist still raised. He lowered it and reached out to shake her dad's hand.

"Hi, I'm Detective Barnes with the Galveston County Sheriff's Office. Is Mrs. Crow home?"

"Hey there, I'm her dad, Thomas Boling." The two men shook hands and came into the living room where they could see Rebecca standing in the kitchen with the phone in her hand. At the sight of the detective, she finished the call and rushed towards them.

Rebecca avoided looking the detective in the eye and gestured towards the couch. "Have a seat. Want some coffee? There's a fresh pot." She walked to the kitchen without waiting for a reply.

Barnes leaned forward and raised his voice so she could hear him from the other room. "I've already had about two pots today. I better not, but thank you."

Rebecca returned to the living room, held her hands together in front of her, and looked around for something to focus on before sitting down across from the detective. She sat on the edge of the couch, tense and uncomfortable.

"Honey, want me to stay with you?"

"No, thanks dad. I'm fine." She met the detective's eyes, "Better go get the food before it gets cold."

"Okay, call me if you think of anything else you need." He grabbed his keys and paused at the front door, looking at the two of them sitting in silence.

"Go dad. And I will, thanks."

Rebecca watched the door close, staring at it long after she felt the detective looking at her, neither saying a word. She turned towards the large window and watched as her dad pulled out of the driveway and headed down the road.

Rebecca was the first to break the silence. "So, did you get him yet?" She returned to her spot on the couch and folded her trembling hands in her lap.

"No ma'am, I'm sorry. There *is…*"

"I saw you on the news the other day…," she interrupted. "A man was killed in a fire?" Her voice broke on the last word and she reached out for her coffee cup. She needed to know if anyone suspected her.

"We're still trying to connect all the pieces. We have another missing man…" He glanced down at his notes. "…Mario Perez." He looked up at her, "Do you know him?"

"No, the name doesn't ring a bell." She shifted on the couch.

Detective Barnes pulled a notebook out of his breast pocket and held out a small picture. It was a formal head shot of a man in a business suit and tie. His head wasn't bald at all, but full of thick salt and pepper hair. Intense hazel eyes stared out from an olive toned face. He was definitely *not* the man Rebecca had killed the day before.

She shook her head, refusing to touch the picture, "I don't know him, what happened?" At least she could be honest about that much.

"His wife reported him missing. Says he went fishing down on the jetties and never came back home. It wasn't very far from where Jon was, so we thought maybe there was a connection." He tucked the picture back into his notebook.

"That's awful, I hope he's okay."

The detective nodded in agreement. "What happened there?" He gestured towards the bandage on Rebecca's left arm.

She covered it with her right hand, "Oh it's nothing, just a burn. From cooking. I'm so clumsy."

"A burn, huh?" his head tilted to the side and his eyes narrowed.

"Yeah, but its fine. It's almost all healed up. Was there anything else I can do for you?" She lifted her coffee mug to steady her shaking hands.

Detective Barnes cleared his throat and lowered his eyes. "There is one more thing..."

Her arms froze, holding the cup inches from her mouth. She didn't dare look at him.

"It's about Jon."

Rebecca held her breath.

"We found..." Barnes looked down at the floor, unsure how to say the next part.

Rebecca knew what he was trying to say. "No," she mumbled.

"I'm so sorry."

Rebecca slammed her cup down on the coffee table and glared at the detective, her eyes threatening to spill over with tears. "Say it. You have to say it."

"We found his body."

29

Tommy's death was all anyone in the Third Ward would talk about. James had thought he was an annoying little shit, but apparently some people really liked annoying little shits. James' mama had worked herself up so much about it, he had to make her sit down and take a break from regurgitating the local gossip of how and why. She was barely breathing in between yelling at him to be careful, and being mad at the world for letting it happen to 'such a sweet boy'.

"Tommy was *good* people! *Good* people, James!" She wrung her hands until they were red.

"I know mama, I know." He continued to pat her on the arm.

He almost regretted killing Tommy. He wouldn't have done it if he had known it was going to be such a big damn deal. You would have thought it was her own son, and not just some guy she happened to know of and be around a few times. But it seemed to have been the blood that broke the camel's back. Or straw. Whatever. People were tired of being scared all the time about where they were going, if it was safe or not. He couldn't tell his mama that she really didn't have anything to worry about, that *he* was the bad guy. Shit, she'd have a damn heart attack. No, it was better to let her worry. It would all blow over in a few days.

He finally got her settled in the big comfy chair in the living room, TV tuned to whatever reality show she was into at the time. She continued to sniffle into a pile of tissues while a large woman on the screen was yelling at a much smaller man, that he had to be her baby's daddy. James shook his head as he sat down on the couch. Too much damn drama. That's why he never kept bitches around very long, they started wanting to talk about futures and houses and babies and shit. Alone, he didn't have to worry about that stuff, he was too busy out there getting it. Making shit happen, without a woman or a big fancy job. It was going to be tight, but he could probably make rent just fine without Tommy, and even maybe buy a new TV to replace that cracked piece of shit. But, that would have to wait. He needed to lay low for a bit, let that van business die down and get some space between him and Tommy's death. Maybe he didn't need to leave town.

"You know, a cop came to see me this morning," his mama said, picking her nose with a tissue.

James froze. "What's that?"

"A cop, came to see me. He was askin' about Tommy, and askin' where you were. I told him I didn't know, that you was prob'ly at work." She smiled up at James, "How's that new job goin'?"

"It's good, mama. Why did he want to know where I was?"

"I don't know honey, hey could you grab me some more kleenex from the closet?"

James handed her the tissues and, unable to get any more information out of her, left irritated. Not with her, she had the world's worst memory, but with that damn detective. His mama couldn't remember the cop's name, but it had to be him. None of the other cops ever messed with him. It was a good thing he had taken care of Tommy when he did.

***

The sun was low in the gray sky as James made his way back to Palmer Street. He slowed down, peering through the windshield wipers that were swishing to the beat of the heavy rain falling around him. He could finally see the house just ahead, a nice red brick one with white trim. One of the gutters was hanging down on the side of the house. Fat ass soccer dad must have been the 'fix-it' one of the pair. He looked like the kind of guy who would try to fix everything, and it would end up more broken than before. James coasted to the edge of the road and put his van in park, leaving it running. He turned off the wipers and watched the wife's house through the pouring rain. A few lights were on, one in the front room where she sat with the detective before, and one further back in the house. He guessed that was probably her bedroom.

Across the street, a few kids jumped in puddles and screamed with laughter as they splashed each other. Forgotten umbrellas blew across the lawn as their mother yelled at them from the front porch to come inside. There were no kids laughing outside the Crow house. All was quiet, though it did look like she had company. There was a white Taurus in the driveway, along with the black Ford that was there the last time he drove by. Maybe it was a gentleman caller, perhaps the old girl wanted to dust off some cobwebs. He wouldn't mind helping her out with that, she was still smokin' hot, even if it turned out she was a little crazy. It was the crazy that did it for him, the girl had style and that was hard to find. Rebecca. That's what the papers said her name was.

He still wasn't totally convinced she had the balls to do what was happening. Soccer moms just didn't do that. They worried about PTA meetings and went to book club and margarita nights with the girls. They didn't kill people. They *really* didn't set them on fire. He smiled to himself; he had to admit whoever did that one had style.

There was still no action coming from the house. The living room curtains were closed, so he couldn't tell if she was banging the dude on the couch or in her bedroom.

Probably in the bedroom. Soccer moms weren't exactly creative. Though she was a special breed of suburban mom, so maybe...

He must have fallen asleep, because at the sound of a door slamming, his head jerked up from his chest and his eyes flew open. Rebecca was walking towards her driveway. That was her, all right. Old enough to know how to treat a guy, but still not quite hitting that middle-aged matronly look. Slim, with long brown hair he could already see draped over his own thighs.

She climbed into the black Ford and pulled out of the driveway, turning left. He slouched down in his seat even though it was hard to see anything through the pouring rain. The rising bulge in his pants would have to wait. He shifted into drive and eased out onto the street behind her.

30

Rebecca *was* glad her dad decided to drive down to see her. She didn't know how she would have gotten through those first few days after Jon's body was found, without him. Since the moment he returned that night with an armload of Chinese take-out, he had handled things. Phone calls, funeral arrangements, police reports... all handled. And Rebecca let him, because she didn't care about any of it. She didn't care about anything anymore. Nothing mattered, and there was no longer a reason to get out of bed. She had gotten rid of the man who killed her family, Jon was no longer missing, and everything was settled.

It wasn't until she was in her room trying to figure out what to wear for the funeral, that it hit her. Her dad found her there, sobbing in a pitiful heap on the floor of her closet. It was all too much, and she was so tired. She wanted nothing more than to sleep for a week straight, and to forget about everything that had happened since that terrible night. But she couldn't. She had to go to her husband's funeral and return to a house that would forever be empty. She had to live with knowing she killed two innocent men. The only thing that kept her from crumbling under the guilt of it all was knowing she had finally taken care of the man that had taken everything from her. She had balanced the scales. Sort of.

She washed her face and walked with her dad back into the living room where he had paused a baking show on TV. The man never baked a day in his life, but in the past when she had pointed that out, he said he would one day. She had rolled her eyes and laughed at him. Walking by the TV, she knew she would never laugh like that again. Nothing would ever be the same. The thin string that had held her in place since Oliver's death, was knowing Jon would come home and they would get through it together. But that string had snapped, leaving... nothing. She poured a large glass of wine in the kitchen and gulped it down in one very long. swallow. But she still felt nothing. Her dad stayed perched on the edge of the sofa and pretended to watch the cooking show, but he wasn't fooling anyone. Every time she moved, he looked at her and held his breath. He knew there wasn't anything he could do to help, so he did what he knew how to do best. He left her alone.

"I'm running to the store; do you need anything?"

"Becky, wait."

Rebecca grabbed her purse, wiped the tears off her face, and headed for the front door without glancing back. The door slammed shut behind her as she rushed to the driveway through the pouring rain. Throwing the car into reverse, she pulled out onto her street and pointed herself towards the bridge. Once on the highway, red and blue lights flashed in her rear-view mirror. She held her breath as the police cruiser pulled up behind her, then swerved around to continue its chase. She sighed. No one was coming to arrest her. At least not then. She felt ashamed for being disappointed. Of course she didn't want to go to jail, but maybe it wouldn't be so terrible. She wouldn't be in that empty house where memories of Ollie and Jon screamed at her from every corner. She wouldn't have to go to work where everyone would tiptoe around and feel sorry for her. Her heart screamed in her chest, keeping time with the 'thunk-thunk' of the windshield wipers, and no matter how hard she tried, she couldn't take a deep breath. Rebecca's head was swimming with frustration, sadness, and wine, until she felt them all overtake her as she finally arrived at the bridge.

There weren't any fishermen, and the stray police tape had long since blown away on the gulf winds. Through the storm, she could almost hear the rumble of cars overhead as she sat in her car with her head on the steering wheel, sobbing. A steady plop-plop of fat raindrops fell hard on the hood, running down the car and into the ground around her. A bolt of lightning lit up the sky, illuminating the bridge and reflecting fiery streaks across the rain-dimpled canal. She turned the car off and jumped out into the mud, her chest heaving in an attempt to draw a full breath. It wasn't supposed to be like that. Her life should be different. She should have a son, and a husband, and a life. Gravel dug into the palms of her hands as she crouched there beside her car, her head down to keep rain out of her face. If anyone had glanced down as they drove across the bridge above her, they would have chuckled to one another assuming she was just another college kid who couldn't hold their liquor. Drank a bit much at the pub, that one did. She wished it were that simple.

Rebecca pulled herself up and tilted her chin towards the sky. Thunder rolled in the distance as rain caressed her face, mingled with her tears and carried both down to the ground around her where they rolled in thin channels toward the edge of the water. She walked the path of the small drainage tracks to the edge of the canal and sat down. Rolling waves kissed her feet as she dangled them over the edge. It was the spot where her whole world had changed. It was the water that had taken her precious boy from her. No, it wasn't the water, but the red headed man that had taken her family. And she doubted she would ever know why. But at least she had done one thing right.

Raymond Rodgers, the news had said. His girlfriend found him after she got off work. She knew he was home, but he wasn't answering his phone or the door, because while they were at the 'see each other every night' stage of their relationship, they hadn't quite made it to the exchanging of keys. His work van was there, so she knew he was inside. It didn't take long for her to see legs sprawled out on the floor from a crack in the curtains. She called the police, who uncovered the grisly scene inside. A bold reporter had found the girlfriend sitting on the curb in Raymond's driveway, away from most of the commotion, and had aimed a camera towards her, broadcasting her grief live to the entire viewing area. Her eyes were swollen from crying, and mascara had tracked down her face. Rebecca felt sorry for her. She knew exactly what she was going through. Well, not exactly, but close enough.

But, then she thought about the kind of woman who would be with a monster like that, and she didn't feel sorry at all. Rebecca only wished she had gotten answers from him, but she supposed it didn't matter. Knowing 'why' wouldn't bring them back to her. She supposed her job was done, and she should go home, say goodbye to her dad, and go back to work on Monday. But the thought of going back to that life took all the air out of her lungs. She just couldn't. There was nothing for her there, not anymore.

Moonlight reflected off the rough ripples in the water, raindrops sparkling into the dark night. It looked so inviting, that water. She wanted to slide down into it and let it carry her away. It was as close as she would ever be to Ollie again, feeling the water against her skin. It could take her, and she wouldn't need to try to figure out the rest of her life. She could just slip away. She had always thought of suicide as a selfish cop-out, but for her there was no one to leave behind. No one to mourn, or to live with the weight of it and wonder if there was anything they could have done. Her dad was barely her dad; Rebecca being gone wouldn't affect his day to day life at all. Sure, he'd be sad, he did love her, but he would be fine. All it would take would be a small shifting of her weight, and she could fall into the water below. It would be peaceful, like the old man at the nursing home. She would just be... gone.

Another flash of lightning lit up the night sky around her. She looked out at the bridge carrying people to their lives; cars, trucks, even a few vans. As she watched, an old white van slid under the street lights at the bottom of the bridge, pulled off to the side of the road, and turned around.

31

Ignoring the traffic rumbling overhead, Rebecca turned again towards the water. The violent storm raged around her, building until you could no longer tell where the rain stopped, and the canal began. Ink black water churned and slapped the bottom of her feet as they hung over the concrete embankment. She shifted her weight forward an inch and held herself there, wondering what it would be like to let go, to slide into that welcoming nothingness.

Wide beams swept around her, highlighting the surface of the water, and she turned around.

It was a van. An old white van. A man stepped out, but left his engine running and his headlights on. Rebecca raised her hand above her eyes and squinted, struggling to see anything in the harsh glare. He jogged over to where she was sitting, holding his head low to keep the rain out of his eyes. She swung her legs out of the water and pulled herself up, better able to see him as he came closer. He was lean in an athletic sort of way, and a little shorter than Jon... was. Where Jon had curly blond hair, the man's was dark and cut much shorter. They were both pale skinned, though the stranger's cheekbones stood out much higher than Jon's had, his face sunken around it.

"Hey there! This rain is really coming down, huh?" He huddled beneath the hood of his jacket and grinned at her. All teeth and no bite.

"Sure," she answered, still thinking of that deep, cleansing water behind her.

The man stepped closer and held out his hand. "I'm James."

Rebecca stared at his outstretched palm. Her mind

was desperately trying to surface from the weight of her earlier thoughts, but she couldn't shake the heaviness. Struggling, she forced herself to reach out and touch his hand.

Screams of laughter carried on the wind towards them, cutting through the thick blanket of rain. A group of teenagers ambled towards them from the closed bait shop down the road. A few held bottles covered with brown paper sacks, the sacks clinging to the bottles for dear life as the rain soaked them, pulling them towards the ground. The kids playfully pushed each other into large puddles, taking turns drinking from the bottles.

The man's smile fell as he realized the kids were headed their way. He continued to squeeze her hand until Rebecca pulled back from his wet grasp, shocked out of her fog by the laughter.

"I have to go." She stepped away from the man and headed towards her car.

"No, don't."

Rebecca turned back to the man, standing there in the rain.

"I... um... can you give me a ride?" His smile returned. "My car has a flat tire. That's why I pulled over here."

She stood there, considering his request and grimaced at the irony of it.

"My phone is dead, or of course I would just call someone else." He held his hands up and grinned in a 'what can you do?' gesture.

In normal circumstances, Rebecca Crow would never have given a stranger a ride. She didn't even give the beggars down on Second Street any change when they accosted her at every intersection. She watched enough TV to know what happened to women who stopped to help people out, even if they seemed innocent at first. But on that dark night, in the pouring rain there under that bridge where Oliver and Jon had died, she just didn't care.

"Sure, whatever." She turned back towards her car without another word.

The stranger who called himself James, followed.

She was thoroughly soaked by the time she climbed back into the driver's seat and clasped her seatbelt. Slamming her car door and putting the key in the ignition, Rebecca was almost oblivious to the man sliding into her passenger seat. She didn't really care if he was there or not. Nothing mattered anymore to her.

Glancing in her rear-view mirror as she turned the car around, she finally spoke, "Where to?"

"Just up that way a little." He pointed to the other side of the bridge. "Thanks again for helping me out, I really appreciate it."

"Sure."

Rebecca inched the car onto the bridge, struggling to see the edges of the road in the hard downpour.

James stared at her expectantly.

"Look, this has been fun and all, but I've got things to do, and you're boring me. I thought you would be... different."

Rebecca's eyebrows furrowed in confusion as she glanced at the man next to her.

"What?" She turned back to the road, squinting through the heavy rain.

"Rebecca, Rebecca. I thought you were a tiger, claws out, trying to play the big boy games. But you're just a little kitten, aren't you? Pathetic."

"What are you *talking* about? Do I know you?"

Her eyes bounced from the man to the road, and back again. The car continued its crawl upwards.

"Who am I? Oh, I think you know exactly who I am. You've been looking for me. And my van."

She continued driving, her eyes steady on the road while her mind reeled, trying to find an answer to the question that was sitting next to her.

"Jesus, I thought you were smarter than this. I'm James. James Porter. I killed your sniveling pathetic husband a few months ago right down there." He looked out of his window, down at the churning water. "Sorry about the kid, really. Didn't know that was gonna happen, but what do you do?"

Rebecca stopped the car halfway up the bridge and turned to stare at him, eyes wide in disbelief. It couldn't be him, it was that guy, Raymond Rogers. The plumber. Unless she had gotten it wrong... again. Maybe the plumber was innocent. Just like the man in the green van, and the guy down at the store. She sank into the soaked leather seat and slouched, her foot heavy on the brake.

"Hey there, no funny business. Keep driving." James leaned forward and touched the tip of a knife she hadn't seen to the side of her neck.

Rebecca was no better than the man sitting next to her. The man that – she choked back bile that had risen to the bottom of her throat. She wasn't scared of the man, or the knife. She was just disgusted at being that close to him.

She lifted her foot from the brake and pressed on the gas, the car continuing its slow trek up the side of the bridge.

"Why?"

"Huh? Oh, I don't know. Needed some cash. Like I said, didn't know about the kid 'till it was too late. Honest mistake."

It was as simple as that. It wasn't personal. He had needed money, and Jon and Oliver were in the wrong place at the wrong time. Because of her. Because she couldn't remember to replace a spare tire. It would have taken just twenty minutes to swing by a tire shop, and she hadn't made the time, kept putting it off until she forgot it altogether. One small thing, and it had started an avalanche. And it was entirely her fault. Not Jon's, the doting dad she'd pushed so far away that he finally gave up on trying to make their marriage a happy one. Not Oliver's, who loved them both so fiercely and without hesitation. Ollie, who didn't know how to swim, who was terrified of going beneath the surface. Rebecca could have looked the rest of her life for the man sitting next to her in the car, but it wouldn't have mattered. Because really, she was the one who had killed her family. It was her fault they were dead.

Hard steel dug into the side of her neck as she glanced at the backseat of the car through the rear-view mirror. He was there, he had come back to her. Ollie with his sunburned cheeks and beautiful smile. Their eyes met and he nodded, then giggled and kicked his feet.

Rebecca slid her left hand down from the wheel and rested it against her side, careful to keep her eyes on the road. They were going forward slowly through the thick rain, and were almost to the top of the bridge. Her fingertips brushed the door handle. James started whistling, looking for a radio station with his right hand, while holding the knife at her throat with his left. Her fingers inched towards the latch.

The smooth tunes of WYJC filled the car, loud enough to mask the 'click' of the doors locking. She brought her left hand back up to grip the steering wheel.

Rebecca turned to James and smiled. His eyebrows rose in surprise, then his face fell into an arrogant grin. She slammed on the gas, turning to the right as soon as she got to the peak of the bridge. The car lurched forward, into the small barrier, sending them both hurtling forward. The knife slipped from his fingers and fell, hitting the middle console and bouncing into the shadows of the backseat.

"Bitch!" James grabbed for the wheel.

Rebecca held on with a strength that surprised even her as she shoved the gas pedal down on the floor as hard as she could. Tires spun against the slippery surface of the road while the front bumper crumpled against the short concrete barrier.

As determined as she was, he was still stronger. She strained to hold on as he pushed the wheel an inch to the left.

The angry storm thrashed violently, almost hiding the squealing of breaks on the asphalt behind them. The back of the car caved in as a truck slammed into them, caught the edge of their bumper, and shoved them up and over the small barrier. For a second, time stood still in the small car as it tumbled upside down over the edge of the bridge. Rebecca and James moved as if through deep water, everything slower than it should have been, pushing against an unseen force.

Then they fell.

As the black Ford heaved through the air above the canal, James tried to scream at Rebecca, but only whimpered. Blood dripped down the side of his head where he had slammed into the windshield. Jagged shards of glass protruded from his scalp, and air whooshed into the car through the small hole in the glass.

Ignoring him, she turned to face the backseat and strained against the seatbelt straps. There was Ollie, smiling at her and reaching out his hand. She took it in hers and squeezed.

They hit the water with enough force to pop the rest of the windshield out into the rushing current, and with it, James' body.

32

"Hey, are you still in town? Looks like the AAA guy is here already, we'll just ride with him. You can meet us at the mechanic shop, it's closer to home anyway."

"I'm not, but I can turn around. They got there fast."

"Yeah, I thought so too. But he's not in a tow truck. This is probably the car service so we don't have to ride with the tow guy. Either way, they really need to invest in nicer vehicles. This van looks like it's about to fall apart. I'll call you back when we're on the road again. Love you."

The gravel crunched under the van's tires as it rolled to a stop ten feet away from Jon. A muscular man with wavy black hair stepped out from the driver's side. As he walked towards the blue Chevy, his intense brown eyes belied the grin on his face. Jumping down from the passenger seat was a shorter man with shaggy blond hair. He wasn't smiling.

The first man held out his hand to Jon. "Hey there, having some trouble?"

"Yeah, are you guys with AAA?" Jon asked as he shook his hand.

"Nope, we were just driving by and saw you stopped here. I'm... Mark, this is my buddy... Cal."

Cal, the shorter man, nodded at Jon.

"I'm Jon. Nice to meet ya, but I should be good. I've got AAA coming, they should be here any minute now."

"Well we don't mind keeping you company 'till they get here, do we Cal?"

The blond man shuffled his feet and shrugged.

Jon glanced back towards the car but wasn't able to

see Oliver from where he stood. Silence filled the space between Jon and the car, where just five minutes ago singing had projected out across the water. Jon hoped Oliver had finally given in to the nap he had been fighting ever since they left the beach.

The brown haired man pulled a cigarette from his shirt pocket, a lighter from his jeans, and held the pack out to Jon.

"No thanks, I quit about five years ago. The wife would kill me if I came home smelling like smoke." He chuckled nervously.

"Oh man, I get it. My old bitch used to hate the smell of smoke, didn't she," he paused and turned towards the other man, "Cal?"

"Oh yeah, sure... *Mark,*" the man assuming the name of Cal grabbed one of the cigarettes and lit it, looking out towards the water as he drew in a long, deep drag.

"Yeah, I never notice the smell but they say you get used to it after a while so who knows... maybe I do stink. Do you think I stink, Jon?"

Jon's eyes narrowed, "Not at all."

"Aw you're nice, isn't he nice Cal?"

"Sure," he mumbled, keeping his eyes on the water.

"Yeah, it's too bad. It's always easier when they're not nice, but what can you do?"

Jon took a step towards his car, but the man calling himself Mark was faster. He darted between Jon and the blue Chevy.

"Where ya goin' man? I thought we were hanging out?"

"Look, I don't want any trouble, and AAA should be here any minute."

"Oh, it's no trouble, no trouble at all." He winked and pulled a knife from his back pocket and flicked it open, the sunlight catching on the sharp blade. "Just give me your wallet and we'll be out of your way."

The shorter man dropped his cigarette and stepped on it. "Dude, just give us your wallet and we'll leave, promise."

"What are we now, the fucking boy scouts?" the taller man sneered at his companion. "You 'promise'? You gonna pinkie swear now?"

"Just get the wallet, we need to get out of here."

"Easy there, you don't call the damn shots. Just calm your tits, we'll be done when I say we're done."

Jon inched backwards while they argued, keeping his eyes on the tall man. He eyed the distance to the car, he knew he would need to go around them to reach Oliver, but he wasn't as fast as he used to be. Too many years of pizza nights and fast food had taken their toll. Just as he was about to make a run for it, the back of his left foot hit the edge of a crumpled coke can, sending it scrambling a few feet across the gravel.

"Where do you think you're going?" the taller man said. "I'm not finished with you. Didn't I say give me your wallet?" He pointed the knife at Jon's jeans and gestured with his wrist.

Jon pulled his worn wallet from his back pocket and held it out to the man. He told himself that it was okay, really. He would cancel the credit cards and bank card, and he could always order another copy of his driver's license and social security card. He should have listened to Rebecca when she told him not to carry that last item around with him. She said *If you ever lose your wallet or get mugged, they have all your information, and who knows what they'll do with it.* She was right, of course. She was almost always right. Well, except when she forgot to put a new spare in the trunk.

The taller man took the wallet with his free hand and

tossed it to his friend. "See how much is in there, will you?"

He rifled through the wallet before answering with a sigh, "Thirty-two dollars."

The man calling himself Mark stared at Jon, "Are you fucking serious with this shit? There's no way you only have thirty-two dollars."

"We... I... went to the beach and bought some stuff... I swear that's all I have." He flinched as the man holding the knife took another step towards him.

"I think he's holding out, Tom-I mean Cal. He's got more, he just don't wanna give it up."

"Man, come on. I believe him, let's just get outta here." The shorter man turned and headed back towards their van.

"Nah, you're holding out. Where's the rest? In a damn sock somewhere? In your car?" Jon's eyes widened at the mention of the Chevy. "I bet it's in your car isn't it? Cal, keep an eye on him, will ya? I'm gonna check this out."

Jon reached out and grabbed the man's arm, needing to pull him away from the car and his sleeping son. The man turned towards Jon, knife still in his outstretched hand, and plunged the sharp tip deep into the soft flesh of Jon's stomach. For a moment, both stared at each other in disbelief. The only sounds were the rumbling of cars overhead and the gentle lapping of the water.

The silence was broken by Jon's scream as he tried to break away, but the man calling himself Mark had a tight grip on him with his free hand. With his other, he pulled the knife out of Jon's stomach before sinking it back in, lower and deeper than the first time. Dark red blood swam in rivulets down Jon's shirt and jeans, saturating both. Jon grunted, a deep guttural sound, and continued the fight to break free. The tall man, finally noticing the blood on Jon's clothing, held him further away from himself, trying to keep his own clothes free of the mess. Jon saw his opportunity and pulled himself free with one final jerk, then ran in the only direction he could, towards the water.

He stood at the edge and turned to look back towards the men. In front of him, the tall man was jogging in his direction. To the left and behind the men was Jon's car. His heart sank as he saw Oliver poke his head up above the window in the back seat. He had gotten out of his booster seat and was watching them, blond curls barely showing in the shadows. Jon made eye contact with his son and pushed towards the ground with his left hand, hoping Oliver would understand and duck out of sight. Before he could turn back to the tall man, it was too late. The hand holding the knife was already arcing through the air towards him. Jon barely registered it out of the corner of his eye before it sank into the soft flesh between his neck and his chin, just to the left of his Adam's apple. He reached up, clutched the sharp edges of the blade with his hands, but was unable to pull it out. He looked into the eyes of the man who held the knife, eyes that were bright with excitement and dull at the same time.

Jon stepped backwards and fell into the water with a small splash. The cars rumbling across the bridge overhead didn't slow down, nor did the boats off in the distance. Only the fish moved to the side as his body slipped beneath the surface. As the current carried him away, his car, and Oliver, drifted out of sight.

Tommy was screaming, "James, what the hell, man? What did you do?! We need to get out of here, *now*!"

"What *you* need to do is calm the hell down, and what *we* need to do is get rid of this car."

"You didn't have to kill him, he didn't even know our real names!"

"It's not like I meant to, Tommy. Now shut the fuck

up and help me with the car." James picked up his pace and hustled towards the blue Chevy.

Tommy followed James, like he knew he would, like he always did. James reached the car first and glanced in the back seat. "There's a kid seat back here, well at least the kid ain't with him. That would be awkward as hell."

"James, forget about the car, let's go!" Tommy whined.

"At least the dumbass left the keys in the ignition, here I've got it in drive... grab that rock over there." Tommy picked up the rock and tossed it to James, a little harder than he needed to. James glared at him before wedging it onto the gas pedal. He shifted the car into drive and jumped out just as the car started to roll towards the water. They both began to breathe a sigh of relief as all evidence of their little... mishap... was about to go over the edge and disappear. Just as the front tires cleared the edge of the embankment and the car started to dip, they saw a small boy's head pop up in the back window. His curly blond hair matched that of the man they had just killed.

"Fuck," they whispered in unison.

James grabbed Tommy as he started to run towards the car. "Let it go, he's seen us anyway, you want to go to jail? 'Cause I don't. Just let it happen, Tommy."

"But... he's a *kid* James! A baby!" He struggled to get free, but it was too late. The rear tires had just cleared the edge and the car was sinking fast. Water was already up to the door handles.

"Let's get out of here." James was halfway back to the van before he realized Tommy wasn't behind him. "Tommy, *now*! We need to leave! There's nothing else we can do!"

Tommy jogged to the van and climbed in without another word. Through the dusty window he watched the car bob in the water as they pulled away.

Oliver whimpered as the water rose in the car, rushing past the front seat and closer to him. He lost his footing from his perch on top of the car seat and splashed down into the murky water. Small arms flailed out and his legs kicked, but he kept sinking into the depths with the car. Memories of an unsuccessful swim lesson surfaced, but he had left before he was able to learn even the basics. Unable to swim to the small air pocket at the top of the car, his throat burned with trapped oxygen and his ears pounded. He opened his mouth to scream again for his dad but water rushed in, pouring down his throat and filling his lungs. Oliver's eyes bulged as he clawed at his throat, trying to breathe. Bubbles gurgled up from his open mouth as he struggled to get to the top of the car, but it was too late. Eyes glazed over, his small body floated to the top of the Chevy, hands still clutching a very soggy blue elephant.

Made in the USA
Coppell, TX
13 November 2020

41211765R10131